Thieves of Time Forgotten

By Emilia Ramos Samper

Thieves of Time Forgotten, The Shadow Heir Trilogy
by Emilia Ramos Samper © 2024

All rights reserved. No part of this book may be reproduced or transmitted in any form or by any means, electronic or mechanical, including photocopying and recording, or by any information storage and retrieval system, without permission in writing from the author.

This is a work of fiction. Names, places, and situations are used fictitiously in this book. Any resemblance to persons – living or dead – places, situations, or other dragons is entirely coincidental.

Warning: unauthorized redistribution or duplication of any content herein is illegal.

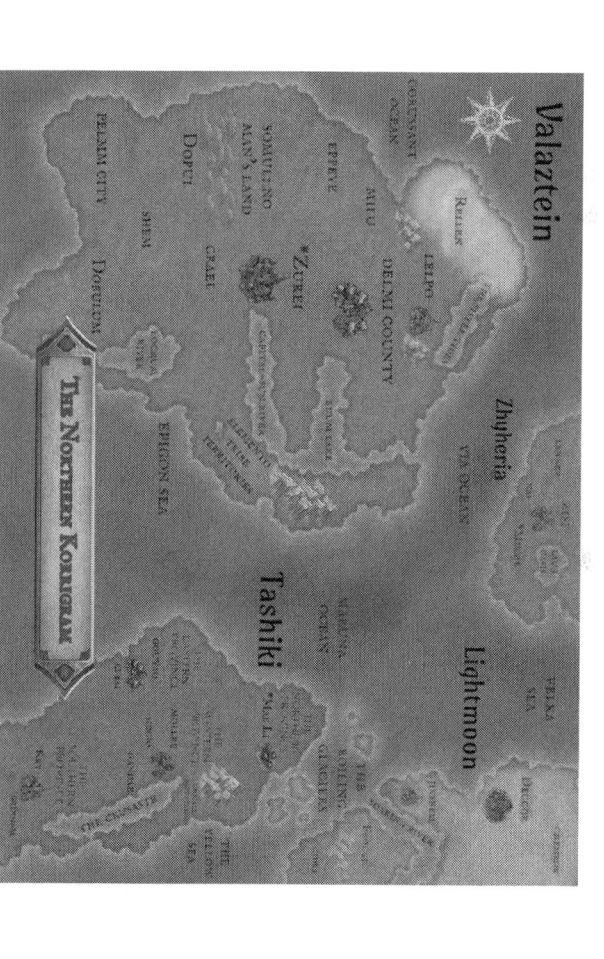

"Dear citizens of Valaztein,

It is with great grief that I must declare the death of my daughter, Princess Naomi. May the gods above bless her soul and may they cleanse her of the evils that took her from us. Today marks the beginning of a new world, one untainted by beasts of scales, blood, and fire. Beside me stand two of my tamed monsters. Ez, Ariah, come forward. These heroic soldiers have joined the forces of light and good, betraying their race of bloody demons and setting forth into a new age of human enlightenment.

Thank the skies, I shall know that my daughter did not die in vain. Her death eradicated the sparks of any revolution in this country. She will not be your martyr; she will not be your hero. My daughter was a foolish, reckless child who chose to play with a government that has endured *centuries*. Tell me now, my good citizens, would you also like to be buried ten feet underground at the ripe age of fifteen?

Didn't think so.

Months ago, Naomi was standing on this very palace balcony, persuaded into a dangerous escape with a Changeling criminal. In the chaos of her escape, my eldest daughter, Naira, died. Naomi went on to the dragon base, even attempting to lead a futile rebellion with the members of the Elemento Tribe Territories.

Oh, children, so naive about the ways of war...

So, take her death as a warning to anyone who dares to challenge the authority of Valaztein. Together, we will grow stronger, tearing down every other nation until Valaztein becomes the greatest empire that has ever lived! Apart, our beautiful country will burn, with every single one of you suffocating in its ashes."

- The Imperial Address: Queen Miranda of Valaztein
Solaris 21, The Day of Shadowed Sun

Prologue

In the fragile light of a chamber consumed by shadows, a broken man fought his queen.

She felt the terror in his presence, battling the ever-present desire.

The desire that singed, eager to set the world afire.

The shadow queen inched closer and continued in a silent whisper.

"I'll give it to you," she breathed down his neck. His icy eyes glared back, no longer cold and unfeeling. No, they now singed with a passion for the one thing that could salvage his race.

"You'd never."

"That dragon is everything."

"I won't give in to you."

"You lie just like him," she recalled, reminiscing about the lips of a past life. The lips of her long-gone love and traitor. "You killed your parents to protect the dragons, and yet now you choose humans over your kind."

"I choose Naomi," the man replied through gritted teeth. She was close; he would break soon.

"You know you're like a son to me, Esmond."

"That isn't my name. Not anymore."

"Then prove it, Changeling." He could fight back, but never would. Not when he stood beside the most powerful queen in the world. Or witch, some would say.

"I have to save Valaztein for Naomi, not just dragons." Those empty words echoed against the walls, each time losing more resilience.

"What about *your* kingdom? What about *your* people? You can right the wrongs you know. Start anew."

"I won't forget who I am!"

"Oh, but you already have." She smirked. "The moment you fell in love with a princess of dark blood."

"What do you want!?" he shouted.

"I want *my* kingdom back," the witch replied, her blackened eyes glittering with greed.

"Give me my Valaztein."

"Why would I ever give you that?" he screamed. But his despair was met with a mere whisper, quiet but impossible to ignore.

"Because without me, your people will wither and die. Because there's only one thing that can save them now:

The dragon heir."

2 Years Later

Chapter 1: Run, Stop, Rewind - (Amethyst)

Kry, Tashiki

Amethyst closed her eyes to the sight of snowy golden palaces and sappy family portraits. *It's always a nice shocker, waking up to Kry's ratty streets and gambling crooks.*

Welcome to the town where hope goes to die.

Amethyst darted right past Kry's signature black market, sliding through the grimy stone floor that always tripped up the royal guards on her trail. *Ah, just another day at work.*

Picking pockets, stealing for scraps… it's not personal, it's survival. When she was younger, Amethyst dreamed that her parents would whisk her off to a far-away palace in the North Province. Hah, what a dumb kid she was… Screw those who lived that dream and screw six-year-old her for thinking she could ever be good enough for a noble family.

For a family at all.

As she dodged between masked traders and sketchy men, the sandy streets morphed into a blur of tarped caravans and forbidden merchandise. After stealing a glance at the guards on her trail, she halted at a run-down wall overflowing with oxidized pipes, a much quicker route to the mandatory tax collection. She never wanted to miss the town throwing cigarettes at the newest palace hire. Oh, how she hoped it was some poor kid from the capital! They always got far more flustered than the sulky middle-aged men who signed up for the job. (Once, one had cried!)

There would probably even be a curfew reinforcement 'cause of the upcoming coronation.

Hopefully not, because the stolen assortment of cologne for Grek's birthday wasn't going to make itself. Perhaps the perfumer's tendency to get caught up in time gaps would scare away the remaining thieves.

As she climbed the peeling scarlet pipes, Amethyst remembered the rumors surrounding them. One of Grek's girlfriends told her people stuffed the pipes with sharpened rocks from the mine.

Realizing that he couldn't climb the pipes with quite as much agility, a guard shot a knife at her. She pulled off a flaky sheet of metal and shielded her face. The pipe didn't disappoint, flowing with rocks that tumbled like an avalanche onto the guards.

Amethyst glared at the jumble of mucky blue uniforms and rocks. Thankfully, none of them appeared to be having any lasting injuries, so she just sighed. She readjusted her tousled bun and black shorts before heading down.

"Stop there, thief!"

Another round of guards ran through the black market, quicker this time. They made their way through the vendor canopies with ease, gaining speed on her. Uh, all this fuss for a stupid pair of earrings!

The pipes got sparser as she made her way up the building, so she focused on her three-step strategy for success. Run. Stop. Rewind. The first part was always the easiest. Check. Then she threw herself over the pipes, landing on a rooftop too in the open to lend her any time. The guards were gaining ground, halfway up the pipes already.

Freaking guards!

Stop was checked. Rewind was next. Amethyst clutched her bracelet and visualized a clock in regular time. Forwards. Forwards. Forwards. A knife landed near her neck.

No, no, no, no...

Focusing on rewinding.

She closed her eyes, anticipating the next knife. The clock was turning counterclockwise now. Backward, backward, backward. It was going faster than she intended, but it was beyond hope that she could control the clock's speed. All she focused on was moving it back.

Another knife landed, cutting off part of her bun. She braced herself for one of two outcomes. The first where she was dead, the second where her weird little abilities had succeeded. A dagger graced her forehead.

Rewind. Check.

Amethyst chuckled when she met Grek at the mucky beer bar on 84th Street, flirting with the mayor's twins. Despite their insistent fiddling, his light brown hair remained perfectly groomed, strangled to perfection by an unnatural amount of stolen hair gel.

"Hey, cow."

Amethyst rolled her eyes. Regardless of her best efforts to steer clear of his annoying nicknames, Grek had deemed her odd hair color worthy of his corny jokes. Amethyst readjusted her bun as the rest of the bar gawked at her strips of pure black and white hair. It was easier to tell people that she had dyed it, yet her hair's origin remained a mystery. Even Kry's stylist had deemed it unfixable.

How does that happen? Ah, it was just another unsolved puzzle from her long-gone childhood. Like the bracelet wrapped around her wrist so tightly it practically cut off her blood flow. It was the only thing she had left of her family, so it getting stolen wasn't an option. Amethyst could just imagine her parents standing there, ready to abandon her on the streets thinking: *Hey, why don't we give her a nice gold bracelet? That'll make everything better.* She should've sold it a long time ago; why keep such an awful reminder?

"No more beer for you," Amethyst said, flicking away the bottle and shooing off the twins.

Grek groaned.

"C'mon, let me have a nice morning." He eyed the bottle furiously, then lunged for it and missed by an inch.

"You've got a real problem," she replied.

"How'd you tell I had one too many?"

"It's not morning." A raven-haired woman passed by their table, searching for pockets in a dress that didn't have any. Like true thugs, Amethyst and Grek quickly spotted the eye-catching gold ring on her finger.

Grek had grown quite a reputation with girls and thievery. It was a long story that not many people understood. At thirteen, Amethyst and Grek had almost starved in Kry. Jobless, dirt poor, and orphaned, Grek asked a girl for food. Maybe it was some charisma that Amethyst was clueless about, but the girl thought he was flirting. After a night out, Grek came back with her wallet. He had continued to do this, and they had continued to not starve.

The end.

"Can you even tell them apart?" Amethyst asked. Her finger pointed at the twins, who were now drinking more cheap wine at the bar.

"I dunno. Can you?" Grek replied.

Searching for a subject of conversation that didn't involve starving, knives, the black market, or stealing, Amethyst was stumped. She finally landed on, "What do you think of the new coronation?"

"I'm pretty excited," he replied, shocking her. "I mean, what if things really did change. Don't you think they could?"

Grek was too hopeful.

"Doubt it," she replied. "It's just another royal baby, and we're here to be his toys."

"Brighten up. We're still here, right?"

"You're right," Amethyst admitted with a sheepish grin. "Though there's not much else to brighten up about."

"The new tax collector's coming soon." Grek pulled out a whiskey bottle from his leather sack.

"That reminds me," Amethyst recalled as she tapped the bottle. "I'm still mad at you for trading the earrings I stole for... that."

"You can have some if you want."

"I'm not feeding your addiction. Besides, we've gotta be on it. Remember that thing called food we gotta steal?" They burst out laughing. What a strange reaction to their dire situation.

"Anyway," Grek continued. "When's the tax collector getting here? I thought he'd show up early. Being his first day and all." Then, the first jeers echoed from the crumbling main road.

"He doesn't disappoint."

Should Amethyst hope people had the civility to put out their cigarettes before throwing them? Well, the late king hadn't when he "temporarily defunded public schools in the Southern Province for national funding." (There had been nothing temporary about it.) No, Amethyst would see his servants crash and burn, just like he'd let his people.

After a few failed attempts at calming the raging crowd, the collector gave up and left, honking his little horn so that people would stop rushing onto the road. He even used his windshield to defend against the rotten apples, but Amethyst was pretty sure one of Grek's throws had broken one of the swipers.

"That one's a fast learner," a man pointed out as the tax collector rushed out of his carriage and ran. Grunts of agreement resonated through the crowd. Through all the commotion, Amethyst almost didn't catch the quiet voice beside her.

"Can you believe that?" The man's golden curls peeked out of a black cloak, not an unusual outfit for the area. "They're all yelling at him like animals."

"Well, it's not like they're gonna pay their taxes." Amethyst chuckled. The man's bright blue eyes widened.

"Why not? Do you pay yours?" His tone was difficult to make out. Not angry, but… curious.

"You're not from around here," she replied. "Plus, with what money?"

"The money from the capital's relief programs," he responded. Amethyst laughed even louder.

"That's cute. Maybe there's also beach cleanups and dependable royal guard services or oh! What about schools?" His face remained blank, even after her rant. Huh, would the cloaked figure respond with a snarky comment or an angry demand? He was a monarchy sympathizer, no doubt, but somehow that wouldn't fit in with his sweet, utterly clueless demeanor.

"That's horrible," the man said, fidgeting with his hood before changing the topic.

"Your name?" It was a fairly odd question, considering half of Kry had fake names.

"Amethyst. Yours?"

"Lodem," he said. "And you should stop stealing. The loop never ends." Wow, he really was adorable. Amethyst caught him staring at her striped bun.

"You're gonna ask what's up with my hair, right?" Lodem nodded and they laughed.

"Did you dye it?"

"No, it's been like that since I was little," she said, surprising herself with the honesty.

"Speaking of which, where are your parents?" Lodem looked around. It was like he expected them to be near her, watching from the closest corner.

"Who knows? Not many people in Kry have any, much less know them," Amethyst replied. He turned back towards her, pity flooding his gaze.

"That—"

"You don't have to pity me. I've got life better than almost everyone here. I mean, I've got a mostly normal friend, poverty hasn't driven me to stupid things, and I know how to steal."

"That's a positive way to look at it." He smiled, and she found herself returning it.

"Actually, I'm an orphan too."

Amethyst reeled back; she definitely didn't have Lodem pinned as the orphan type. So, she asked, "Do you miss them?"

"My mom," he replied. "Just my mom. Do you miss anyone?"

"Well, I don't remember my parents, so my friend Grek is really the only family I have. I don't know what I'd do without him."

Amethyst sighed, glad that she didn't remember losing the people she loved like Lodem. Grek had lost people, too. He used to live in Valaztein until his little sister was stolen away in the night, a memory that still haunted him.

"Well, I should head back." Lodem started walking towards the main road, but Amethyst followed.

"Wait." She slipped a combat knife out of her pocket. "So you don't get killed."

He inspected the little dagger like it was rare, and Amethyst realized that where he came from it probably was. Finally, he grabbed the handle and said, "Thank you."

"You're holding it wrong." Amethyst giggled a little as she corrected his grip, sliding her fingers between his to move his hold. "Good luck."

Before she could make another comment, Lodem chatted with a nearby street seller and finally agreed on something.

Lodem tossed her a small chain hooked to a stone, and she was barely able to spare a glance before he said, "You too." Just like that, her mysterious and handsome cloaked man disappeared behind a corner. Amethyst stared at the necklace, scoffing.

A pure gold chain and an amethyst jewel. She should've set her sights on his wallet, not his lips.

She returned to the main road, only to realize that she was grinning like a fool in the reflection of a puddle. What had gotten into her? A few moments afterward, she felt the familiar beat of her heart accelerating, her brain about to explode. No! Not this again! Her breath raced.

Oh no, no, no, no…

She shoved through the blur of people in front of her, more dazed by the second. She screamed frantically before collapsing on the ground.

"Grek!"

The last thing she heard was his familiar voice as the world plunged into darkness.

Chapter 2: The Only Way Out - (Naomi)

```
Zureī, Valaztein
```

Naomi scoured for any signs of light as she trudged through the scarlet mud, her calf aching. Shoot, was it bleeding?! The dark, musty cave impaired her vision, making the whole world seem somber and blackened.

Another cramp burst through her neck, and her burns shrieked for attention. But Naomi couldn't spare a second glance. If her mother watched this, she wouldn't give her the satisfaction. Hopefully, Ez had already killed that witch. Not really caring if it made her a terrible person, Naomi almost slid into a smile. If not for her bruised jaw, she probably would've.

There was a familiarity to the darkness, like that of an old friend. Actually, a few friends had come to visit: shadows. Quiet, hidden creatures that changed faces in an instant. Some days they watched over her, yet other days they tormented her. But still, they weren't her mother's shadows. No, these strange beasts of the dark belonged to her.

And on the days with no shadows, Naomi wondered. About love. About war. About escape. What would it feel like to have light, warmth, and fire? Maybe she'd crawl away, or perhaps she'd relish it like before.

But nothing was like before.

If she kept saying that, would she start to believe it? Probably not. For some reason, her nature consistently leaned away from reality and into hope. Well, some things hadn't changed from when she was a weak little princess. At least hope ensured she'd keep fighting to get out.

But it also made it that much harder at every dead end.

On those rare nights when she slept, the same nightmare crept through her dreams. In that odd life, she'd never pushed Ez, she'd never jumped into the Maze, and she'd never lost him.

Somehow that painless, easy life... was so much worse than this because of Ez.

So every waking moment of every waking day, she repeated the same few lines:

My name is Naomi.
I'm alive.
Ez is alive.
My people are safe.

And she stayed sane, somehow. No stopping. No crying. No giving into the pain. No matter how much her bones ached, her muscles cramped, and her skin bled, she couldn't surrender. Because if she did, then everything was truly lost.

Light.

With it came time, whereas with darkness came chaos. No real-time, no sense of place, just a sliver of light peeking through a crevice in the Maze's walls.

She sprung out of her seat when she saw that tiny, hopeful crack. Worried using her powers with so little energy could kill her, she hit it with her hand. Naomi punched the wall, desperate and determined. Slowly, it came crumbling away. The hole became an escape route, and Naomi chased the light. She crashed through the hole, but the sun betrayed her.

It blinded her.

Hello, light. It's been a while.

Naomi closed her eyes, stumbling back. When she opened them, not even her purple jaw could stop her from grinning. What year was it? How many years had she lost in real-time? Did she want to know? Before Naomi found her bearings, a stream of assurances flowed out of her.

The Queen and Ariah were dead or locked up somewhere. She'd see Ez and cuddle with Miko. Finally, Naomi could glimpse the faces of her people. The people she gambled everything for. Oh, the world would return her *happiness*. That scared little girl would find the home she suffered for. She'd see the end of her story.

But then Naomi found herself in the palace sewers, which were still intact and boobytrapped. She held onto her last fleeting breaths of hope as memories of slow torture glared back at her. Naomi still remembered each and every one of the hidden traps surprisingly well.

Why was she surprised, though? Torment like that never goes away.

When she reached the end of the sewers, Naomi stumbled into a room that had been horrifically repurposed.

The palace was still in use because nothing about the room was unkempt or abandoned.

The gold-rimmed walls hadn't faded or crumbled; they'd been painted black. The hanging metal cages held petrified animals and appeared newly cleaned, judging by their unnatural shimmer. However, the maids had forgotten to scrub the scarlet stain on the entrance carpet. Beside it lay a familiar tuft of cerulean fur.

"Miko!" Naomi cried out. Sure enough, his high hoot followed her voice. Naomi almost burst into tears, relieved at the sight of him. "He's alive," Naomi whispered to herself. "He's alive." That was before she saw the empty space next to him. Wasn't Eleora, his wife, there with him? He wouldn't have left her except if…

Miko shook his head. *Dead*.

"Let's go," she said, banging on the little cage door. "Does this thing need keys?" Miko merely rolled his eyes at her.

"Okay, okay, where are they?" Miko pointed to a shelf and then put up two fingers with a wave of his right hand.

"Second cupboard on the right?" Miko nodded, but she couldn't get a smirk out of him or anything. The little snow monkey used to giggle at everything.

Naomi grabbed the key labeled "Blue Monkey" and unlocked the cage. He crawled up her arm, devoid of life and spirit. After unlatching all the cages and guiding the animals through the vents to freedom, Naomi and Miko finally passed through the next door.

What new terrors would await her now?

"No," Naomi whispered to herself. "I'm going home. I'm seeing Ez. It's gonna be fine."

But alas, it was only a whisper in a palace full of screams. Naomi didn't even notice she was choking Miko until he wiggled around in her arms, gasping for air. Releasing her grip, Naomi sighed.

They'd make it out fine. Ez was fine.

Quivering, Naomi opened door after door. Every room was perfect and organized, yet cold and terrifying. She even caught a small glimpse of one of the maids but didn't dare speak. Instead, Naomi followed her, keeping steps and breaths coordinated to avoid being caught. She almost forgot to hide when the maid entered a dark chamber with another woman. Naomi eavesdropped on the conversation from her corner behind the wall.

"But, Black Queen"—Who the hell was the Black Queen?—"the Crown Maze detection devices don't show her—"

"What is this incompetence? Find her at once. I don't care if you have to send the whole world there to do it." Ariah.

No, no, no, no, no. Ariah should be dead or locked up somewhere! No, dead. Much better dead.

"Oh, that won't be necessary," another voice responded, all too familiar. "Come out, Naomi. I can feel you."

Miranda. Naomi stood, shaking. It took several moments to process the situation and at least a few more seconds for the world to stop pivoting. By then, yet another voice was speaking, distracting the Queen.

"Your Highness, what happened?" Ez. Why would it be Ez? How could it be Ez? Unless... All the pieces fit together. Ez was the only one who could've brought the Queen back to power because he had the people's trust. He had Naomi's trust.

But...

"Come out, Naomi," the Queen repeated. "I won't ask again."

It was her way to taunt; a part of Miranda's plan to transform her into a helpless little kid again. But Ez had already done that. How many would he kill to satiate his greed? His parents, Eleora, the people! What happened to them; were they brainwashed, tortured... killed? Or worse, had they become the Queen's black magic guinea pigs? All because of Ez, what he did, and what he'd do.

But anger came in waves.

Denial.

He didn't do this. He couldn't have. Ez would never betray me.

Sadness.

But...how could this be happening?

Fear

What happens now?

Vengeance

He'll pay. Or die.

Naomi didn't want to face Miranda, not then. Not if she could help it. She sprinted through the gloomy halls of the palace, not even flinching at the Queen's frantic orders to kill her. Tears dripped on her shirt.

"Stop it!" she yelled at herself, but the tears kept coming. Because her story was not ending any time soon, no matter how desperately she wished it would. Ha, she thought the world would let her win! The villagers never died at the hands of the evil queen, and certainly not because of the hero. Could she even call herself that? Only villains should die, yet her mother never seemed to fall flat.

The familiar scent of dusty carpets hit her as Naomi sprinted through the rooms she used to know. Once they were overflowing with life, gold, jewels, and promise. Now... all the extravagance was just another sick reminder of what she owed her people.

Maybe she should give in and end it all! Maybe dying was the right choice. At least she'd be with Infitri, Gin, Naira, Eleora, and the sweet kids from Eppeye and the Changelings she couldn't protect and... her dad. They'd all be there for her, waiting.

She had the power to finish it now. Why was she their savior? She wiped her face, damp from tears and sweat. She'd done a terrible job protecting her country and just managed to get more people she loved killed. As she reached the golden dining hall, guards surrounded her, pushing her towards the edge of the room. There was nowhere to go, nothing left to do. Then, Naomi saw the crystal windows in front of her.

She rushed right into them, sending sparks of glittering crystals into the air and her skin.

They cut at her face, giving way to tomorrow's new scars. The freefall knocked the wind out of her. Besides, her heart was too empty for screams anyway. The view below her was as beautiful as ever: a royal blue moat leading into the frosted cobblestone streets of Zurei.

A moat that she was about to hit. Her legs numbed as they hit the ice-cold water, and the rest of her body followed suit. As she sunk to the bottom, Naomi let her thoughts win. *I could stay here forever.*

I could let the cold kill me, or the water, or both. No more pain. No more betrayal. Just this numbness.

Miko tugged at her shirt collar, urging her to get up.

Miko. He meant something. All the people who died did too. They still did. And, yes, she felt at fault for their deaths, so now it was her burden to carry. If Naomi couldn't continue their fight, they wouldn't mean anything. They never would've.

Naomi swam out of the moat and kept running, not because she believed she could fix things, or because she thought she could be happy, but because it wasn't her choice to make. It was that of the people who she'd failed to save. So she'd burn, but not before she turned Ez and the Queen to ashes in her fire.

Back then, Naomi was just a little girl who gave her heart away. And Ez had traded it to a monster. Now, as Naomi saw the truth for the first time, as she viewed what had become of that little girl's heart, blackened and broken, she would never give her heart away again. People say that the eyes are a gateway to the soul. Well, she should've known from the first day she saw Ez's eyes in those air vents. Ice-cold eyes, ice-cold heart.

Agony flooded her body as she used her powers, but soon after came the wrath, the fuel, the power. And every space where her tears had fallen burst into shadowy flames. It truly was a gut-wrenching explosion.

Naomi took the trembling in her bones and transferred it to the ground. Everything behind her crumbled; the guards with it. Without a second glance at the lives she had ended, Naomi kept running. Because at that moment, she too was broken, clueless as to how to put the pieces together.

Chapter 3: The Thief and the Jewel - (Urumi)

Kry, Tashiki

Urumi strode past another of Kry's black markets, characterized by the scent of sulfurous gems. Weren't forbidden markets like that supposed to be hidden? Uh, why was he even here? This whole outing was a catastrophe. What prince in his right mind would tour highly dangerous provinces right before his coronation?

Two glaring red eyes scouted him out from under a brown hood, cold and eerie. Feeling exposed, Urumi pulled down his cloak further. If the girl, Amethyst, had figured out his foreignness so effortlessly, who was to say others wouldn't?

She's different, he thought. *She has to be. Why would someone like her be among those thieves and smugglers?* Dear gosh, where was his mind swirling off to? This had to stop. Either way, it wasn't like he would ever see her again. For some inexplicable reason, the thought dispirited him.

Urumi continued to walk down the long street, his pace quickening at the tenth sharpened knife he'd witnessed that hour. *It was the man with red eyes.*

Kry was a strange town, full of strange streets and strange people. Everyone donned hoods, masks, and disguises like their own faces. In every searing, dusty corner, something sinister lurked. This became evident as he walked down the dirty cobblestone road downtown, rushing away from the hooded man.

Slow down, was the first thought that popped into his mind. After all, it was what he had been taught every day of his life back home. If you run, there is something to fear, and if you're safe, then why fill yourself with the illusion of fear? He halted.

That was all the encouragement that the scarlet-eyed thief needed. He leaped towards Urumi, the sharp blade of his dagger glimmering in the merciless Tashiki sun. Urumi sprinted away from the criminal. And twenty-three years of being told to slow down couldn't stop him from running. But then Urumi noticed the strange movement of his clock.

"No." He stared at his silver watch. After what happened years ago… Well, Urumi was more prone to check the time. He scrutinized his watch what seemed like every second of every day, because he couldn't save her from those lethal time gaps, but he could save himself.

Time gaps mostly happened in the Southern Province, his current location, so his feet quickened. As if he could outrun his memories.

Oh, a guard tower! Finally, something safe and civil. The cloaked thief had long since given up, but Urumi kept going. When would the time gap arrive? He desperately pulled at the door of the guard tower, but it didn't budge.

He couldn't die like this. Not like she had.

"Please!" he cried out. "Please, please help me!" His palms dripped with sweat, and Urumi felt his watch slipping off his wrist. As the world danced around his vision, the prince screamed at the door. "LET ME IN!"

The guards didn't open the door, but he could hear the extravagant music coming from the top of the tower. A party. Why in the crown's name were they having a party? He glanced at his watch, a jumbled burr of numbers changed by his stressed vision. That was it!

He shoved open the door.

Gosh, not a kind move for his shoulder. Urumi hurried up the spiral staircase. The moment he reached the top, he ripped off his hood and revealed his golden blonde curls, shouting, "My name is Prince Urumi! I will be your king in thirty days ti—" His vision blurred as the world began to run in circles. Ah shoot, Lai was going to kill him when he learned of this little outing.

And then he fainted.

Mae Lì, Tashiki

Urumi awoke to the silver-lined walls of the palace infirmary. The touch of silky sheets, the scent of flowers and freshly fallen snow... this was home. Mae Li, the capital of the Northern Province, bloomed with flowers resistant to the harshest winters and aristocrats resistant to even harder ones. Urumi looked at his infirmary room and couldn't have been more grateful.

A cotton blanket wrapped around him, soft like a cloud. The scent of flowers came from the baby blue lilies resting on a table beside him. They carried a note, but Urumi couldn't make out the letters. For a few moments, he just melted into the room, not a care in the world.

That was until Advisor Lai barged through the door. Urumi half-groaned and half-smiled. When he was a kid, his mom died and his father shattered into a million pieces. That husk of a man didn't clean up his mess of a mind, not even for his son. Lai had stepped in as dad. And though that meant Urumi was delighted to see his face, it also meant there was a lecture coming.

"Lai..." Urumi muttered, still surprised he hadn't been reprimanded.

"You know that what you did was very foolish."

There it was.

"Yes," Lai continued. "The coronation is in a mere thirty days!"

He nodded like a puppy, not strong enough to deal with this conversation today. "I know."

"Before I go into further detail about your idiocy, I'd like to ask why?"

Urumi answered by repeating something Lai had told him a long time ago.

"How can a king don a crown without knowing those who crafted it?"

"My dear boy, you are wise beyond your years," Lai said. "But why not ask the palace to arrange you a trip? It would've been much safer."

Urumi scoffed. "You would never have let me go."

"And you know this so clearly, how, may I ask?"

Two nurses shuffled into the room, giggling about attending to the young prince of Tashiki. They must have been annoyed when

Urumi didn't even spare a glance, but he had more pressing concerns at the moment.

"Because I haven't left this palace in more than ten years," Urumi murmured under his breath.

"What was that, young man?" Lai glared at him before returning to his calm nature. "Now, answer my original question, like a prince."

"If I had gone with a million guards, I wouldn't have learned anything. No one prepares for a peasant. They do for a prince."

"And did you learn something?" It was a question Lai asked Urumi after every lousy meeting and terrible encounter. It was funny how no matter how high the stakes got, things between them never really changed.

Oh, how he hoped they never would.

"Yes. I learned just how much I owe these people."

Lai smiled. "You're gonna make a great king one day, Urumi. I wish she were here to see it."

Urumi picked up his latest read and chuckled at the title: *The Thief and the Jewel*. Those words reflected his entire morning.

A beautiful thief, he thought.

Urumi flipped through the first few pages of the leatherback novel, unimpressed. He was done with the book in an hour, frustrated that the love interest was another seductive brute. Were there any men left in works of literature who appreciated a well-tailored suit?

As he walked out of bed to stretch, the door creaked open.

No!

He leaped back into bed. If people knew he'd fully recovered from his fainting spell, Urumi would have to continue planning his father's funeral. What was even so mournful about that death, anyway? A horrible king was out of office, and Tashiki now had an opportunity to run itself out of the ground his father had driven it into.

Still, Urumi would feign sorrow; that was how things worked in the court. The aristocrats of Tashiki would do everything in their power to keep the ceremony as superficial as possible. What a waste of time.

A young blonde nurse stepped through the wooden doorway, barely five feet tall.

"Hi, I'll be taking care of you." She checked her blue clipboard, fluttering through the pages to find the right one. "What do you remember before you passed out?"

"I was in Kry. There was this man chasing me. He had a knife."

This was ridiculous. A million different nurses had already asked him this same question. Why would the answer change after his tenth therapy session?

"Do you remember anything after that?"

Urumi rubbed his hand through his hair, a nasty habit that always tangled those blond curls. "A little, but it's a bit foggy."

"That's alright."

"My watch started turning, but it was going too fast. It made no sense, so I thought it was a time gap. I ran to the guard tower, but—I'm not sure if I got there."

"Did you have any disturbing images, something that happened in your past, maybe?"

"A few."

"I'm sorry, Prince Urumi, there was no time gap. Your watch broke and your body's stress systems reacted with some traumatic memories from the loss of..." She halted. No girl in the world wanted to tell her prince that he had mommy issues. "You've been diagnosed with DRD."

"What?"

"Distorted Reality Disorder."

"I know what DRD is!" Urumi shoved his face into his palms. How could this be happening? *DRD. DRD. DRD.*

The day of the funeral soon came, and not even the dessert banquets and chocolate tarts could distract Urumi from the past few days. Every medical record of his condition had been wiped clean, and he, Lai, and the nurse were the only people who knew about his condition.

Nevertheless, that didn't stop Urumi from picturing what might happen if the press got their hands on those records. Tomorrow's headlines would read: *Is Tashiki's New King Up for Ruling? Take a look at his medical files and decide for yourself!* Uh, what a disaster! Tashiki didn't need another unstable king.

He attempted to focus his attention back on the task at hand. Lai had done a great job decorating the funeral and setting up events. The booths themselves were a dull fade of gray, white, and black, while the cakes were dark chocolate. The vanilla cupcakes were disguised with blackened frosting and even the macarons, usually bursting with a rosy color, were all black licorice. The palace played the grieving family's role spectacularly.

You know what they say: fake it 'till you make it.

Now all Urumi had to do was sit in his gray velvet chair with a humble face and a soaked handkerchief. Afterward, he'd deliver a tear-filled monologue detailing how the kingdom of Tashiki would miss his father, the poor, late King Jiko. R.I.P.

Urumi nearly groaned as another pretty lady came to lie about how sorry she was for the loss of his father. Her fluttery pink dress couldn't help but make Urumi think of Amethyst, of how gorgeous she would look in it. *Amethyst.* How was she? She lived in such a different world from his, a world he knew nothing of. The pink-dress lady tapped his shoulder and curtsied.

"Prince Urumi." She smiled. "It's a pleasure to make your acquaintance. I do say, you look rather ravishing for being in mourning."

Ravishing? Who in their right mind would say that at a funeral? A few servers passed by with champagne and he snatched a glass. "Aren't you rather young to be drinking alcohol?" the lady said.

"And here I was thinking you too old to throw yourself at me like a child." Urumi passed her the champagne and strolled around the party.

The flirty winks and sympathetic comments were merely pitiful, albeit annoying. They all thought they had a chance, but they'd soon realize that he would never, ever marry them. What was the point? Why love at all when losing it can leave you so scarred?

Love could destroy him, as it had his father. And then where would his people be? Urumi wouldn't disappoint his country. It was his job to protect it, and he couldn't fail. Not like his father had.

His pathetic, lousy, horrible father.

The man who destroyed Tashiki.

The man who destroyed his family.

The man who had an entire celebration dedicated to his death.

People like Amethyst had been desecrated by his father. Her life's misfortunes could all be tied back to his family's mistakes. Did she worry about starving? Where were her parents? Did she even have any? Was it all his fault for not doing anything sooner? The day he donned that crown, her suffering would end.

But until then, could he sneak out and find her again?

No, just the thought was foolish. Because if he was going to help her, and everyone else like her who needed him, princely excursions, pretty girls, and disobeying orders had to end.

He was a king-in-waiting now.

And she would hate him because he was rich when she was poor, he was safe when she was in danger, and he was full when she was starving.

Urumi kissed his father's coffin and whispered a silent message in a dead man's ear:

"You don't deserve my tears."

Chapter 4: Snake - (Ez)

Zurei, Valaztein

Ez fell at the pace of lightning, every second inching him closer to the marble ground below him. Death seemed like a child's toy now, though he knew it shouldn't have. He still had people to protect and races to save. This was not a game. Death was not a viable option.

What an idiot to even think of it.

But he didn't whisper his incantation just yet, because that selfish part of him wished he didn't have to keep hurting the people he loved to protect them. As he fell from his room in the palace, the adrenaline overtook everything. For just a second, the shock of the cold and the fall cleared his mind. Crazy to think that the same kid who used to find adrenaline in everything now needed a hundred-foot drop just to clean his mind.

The moment passed, and his thoughts drifted to Naomi. The way he had hurt her was… unforgivable. If she were to ever return from wherever Miranda had sent her, he would no longer be a friendly face. She despised him, another consequence of his lousy choices.

But Ez could always dream. This lovely reality was pointless and fleeting, but for a moment, they were on the outskirts of Milu again, the buildings of his past far in the distance, Naomi in his arms. The cool breeze swooshed in the evening air, and yet Naomi's grin reflected a gentle warmth. With her warmth fleeting, everything went numb with cold again. He froze back into the world where he belonged. Of solitude, of service, of pain. Survive, kill, freeze your pain. Survive, kill, freeze your pain.

He should never have let anyone invade the glaciers of his mind; they were the only things shielding the flames that lived beneath.

Oh, but they were out now.

So, Naomi hated him; she hated what he had done. Ez should've known that she would never want to see him again the moment he chose to protect the dragon heir over Valaztein.

His one purpose. The one anchor to his culture, his family, and his past. He loved Naomi, but his time with her had taken away something else.

His dragons. His home. The only place where he could ever be accepted for himself.

Ez shivered as more snow fell and looked at the blade of his silver dagger, now coated in ice. Hello, winter. Gardeners waved at him from the frosted treetops of the palace. The first few times he did this, they screamed. But now, everyone in the palace was accustomed to these kinds of things. Ariah would try to beat the pain away, to fight and train until there wasn't any energy left for her to think.

They'd both found ways to numb their brains. And on the days that nothing worked, at least they knew it was a fair punishment for their decisions.

Ez didn't so much as flinch at the drop. Whoa, maybe he should be a little more worried than that. His thoughts wandered to

Naomi again, but he let out a quick, icy breath and forced his mind to move on. He had to focus on what was important, finding the dragon heir and protecting his race.

It was all he could do now.

Ez had done everything Miranda asked of him, and now it was the Queen's turn to honor her side of the deal. He knew the dragon heir was in Tashiki now, and Miranda shouldn't have let that slip. Either way, he had already lost too much to care whether she gave her blessing. That evil witch had already made him wait two years, and Ez had no intention of waiting another second.

One day, there would be a world where his life consisted of falls like this. Here, he soared through the sky, in free fall above the entire world. He was with his dragons. He was at home.

But he didn't remember home having a merciless charcoal sky that threw knives of hail at whoever was idiotic enough to challenge it. Home was gone now, but he had to try.

As the ground grew nearer, more thoughts crept in. Thoughts of not transforming, of letting the ground crush his bones to sand, of allowing everything to disappear.

No, whispered a voice in his mind. *Not today.*

Today he had a job to do and a race to save.

Ez whispered his transformation incantation a few feet before hitting the ground. A long breath escaped him as he flew around in the cloudless sky, not caring if every one of the Queen's minions was watching him. Light sparkled off from his scarlet scales in every direction, and the familiar sound of leathery flapping wings comforted him.

It was just like the time Ez and Naomi escaped the palace. Did he have more sanity then or now? Probably then, even if the cannons had made him go ballistic. Gosh, he had been so sure that it would be the last time he ever set foot in that palace. If only he had the stakes low enough to be that naive now.

With a sigh, Ez headed towards the window and transformed just soon enough that he wouldn't bang his head on the icy castle exterior. How horrible did this world have to be for him to know that the upcoming dinner with Ariah and the Queen would be the best part of his day?

The gloomy dining hall led to a table full of knives.

Literally.

Queen Miranda and Ariah discussed the best hilt and blade for the palace's private army, shuffling through thousands of lethal weapons. Well, at least it was better than the day Miranda had tried out poisons on the maids.

"How was your day, Esmond?" the Queen asked from the head of the mahogany table. Her golden heels rested on the crimson carpet. Its dye reminded him of blood. She wore an aureate dress that graced the floor. Huh, her stylist was truly incredible if he could conceal her wicked nature behind cherry-red lipstick and golden gowns.

"Fine," he replied.

"Have you killed yourself yet?" Ariah urged from the other end of the table. Unlike Miranda, she wore no makeup, and her hair was trimmed in a short afro because of its convenience. "You mutter her name in your sleep, you know. I can hear it from down the hall." Naomi had been reduced to vague pronouns by Ariah.

"Your devil is showing," Ez replied.

Ariah scowled.

"I can't seem to find your angel, either, White Joker," Ariah snapped. "Maybe a map would help?" she continued.

Shadows blasted out of the Queen's fists and hit their chests. No one made a sound, but Ez and Ariah glared at each other with blatant fury.

Apparently, time doesn't heal all wounds.

"Ariah, tomorrow you'll be assassinating a rogue member from my advisor's cabinet," the Queen said. "He's spreading rumors that Naomi is alive, and I don't want a soul to believe their martyred rebel princess is coming back for them."

"Advisor's cabinet?" Ez interrupted, chuckling. "I didn't know you still had those."

"And also," the Queen continued. "Try to think up a more creative story, will you? Three fires in a week?"

Ariah groaned.

"Another one? Can't you find something more entertaining for me to do?"

Was she insane? What about murder could possibly be *mundane?* Well, this was Ariah: the girl who had murdered her own mother and betrayed her family. And somehow... Naomi's aunt. The relationship was odd, especially because of dragon and human skins.

Back at the dining table, Miranda said, "I'll find something different for you when you do your job correctly. And a student of my army ran away. 8024 or something."

Ez gulped. *8024.* He'd trained that agent, he'd broken her, and then he'd struck a deal to save her forever. Idiot girl had to drag her friend along with her... Poor guy; he ended up with a face full of scars.

As Ez shuffled through the table's knives, a pang of guilt struck him. These soldiers were just kids. He was picking out a child's weapon for murder. Well, it's not like he was many months above eighteen anyway. Even worse, Miranda said that Ez and Ariah had inspired her newest program: an elite force of teens that killed in the shadows.

Such passion, she had told them. *Nothing like the fire of a child who still believes they have a future.*

Too bad Ez's fire had suffocated a long time ago. Along with his future.

Still, he did what he could: turning children into soldiers. Just like Ez, they had been robbed of everything. Their childhoods, their families, their freedom... all gone. But teaching them to fight? That was something he could give them.

8024's friend (Zyon was his name) was caught by palace guards before he could escape. If it weren't for Ez, his body would still be lying on that field, surrounded by blood-soaked grass. After Ez finished with him, Zyon was one of the most skilled fighters in the world. No guards would ever lay a hand on him again.

One day, those kids would be strong enough to stand up to Miranda, just like Ez had. But this time, they would win.

"I'll take care of finding her," Ez replied, but he wouldn't. A deal was a deal. And he had more important things to do. For one, the dragon heir.

"Alright."

He'd spent years waiting for Miranda to help him find just that: the dragon heir, the key to saving his people.

"I'm leaving for Tashiki," he said. "I'm going to find the heir, and you can't stop me."

Uh, why had he said that? The table hushed, and Miranda laughed. No, it was more of a cackle. Pretty fitting for a witch.

"You act as if you had a say in the matter."

"I do."

"An opinion, yes, but a say, never. You give yourself too much credit. You'll go when *I* decide you do." Ez curled his fists, his next defense cocked and loaded on his tongue. "Besides," the Queen continued, "I have a more important job for you to do."

"And that is?"

"Track down the princess for me, will you? And find a way to kill her."

"Wow," Ez scoffed. "I'm surprised you're letting me out of your sight."

"Dear god no." The Queen laughed. "I just need a few ideas, that's all. Places she might be."

"Screw you! I'm not listening to another word, and the only blood on my hands will be yours." He slammed a knife on the floor, watching its hilt shatter in silent, lethal anger.

Calculated. Quick. Planned. "Don't pick that one for your army of underage slaves."

He walked away from the table, leaving behind the perfect mess. The Queen remained taciturn, but the threats would soon come.

"Clearly you don't care about your life, so I will kill every remaining person you love until you do." Ez flinched. Of the people he loved, very few were left in this world.

And somehow, they still made him weak.

Ez walked down the palace hallway that led to his room. Pure fury and disdain for Miranda were at war with his rational sense. Breathing heavily, he gritted his teeth.

What was wrong with her!?

That stone-hearted psychopath!

Wait! Was that... Miranda's office? Empty. Unlocked. Why? Well, it didn't matter. An opportunity had opened up to examine the scars of a murderer. What had made her so dark and wicked in the first place? What secrets lay deep in her mind?

He crept through the iron door. Letters and books covered her desk, ridiculously unorganized for someone as practical as Miranda. The walls and floor were black with iron designs, like a cage meant for a lightless monster. A massive metal cabinet was shoved to the side, its pearly quality reflecting the few dim lights in the room, all hews of purple, a trademark color for dark magic.

He shuffled over to the cabinet, straining to pull open a drawer. Shoot, they were locked. He mustered up a sneeze, letting the fire explode from his nostrils. A grin slid up his face as the golden flames melted the lock right off. *Nothing like dragon fire.*

The objects lying in those cabinets were daunting within themselves: skulls, potions, and half-burned royal documents... but there was no time to get distracted. Ez kept shoving open the drawers until he finally found his prize gem. A gold amulet with a glittering scarlet gemstone.

On the back, not only did it have instructions, but also an odd puzzle.

Thieves of Time Forgotten

Use this charm at rainbow's light to find It, foe or friend.
Follow the order from red to plum to reach your travel's end
To embark is to leave for a land of thieves and magic, beware
Find Its blood and place It on this gem's glare
To rebirth the genes of a tree nearly bare
Welcome to the hunt of the dragon heir.

Ez slipped it in his hand, more than ready to get out of Miranda's hellish office.

But... something glimmered in the iron. An indigo light faintly reflected on the metal. Did Miranda have a chandelier or something? No. The only light came from candles around the room.

Actually, the indigo light came from behind him. There was a door hidden at the back of the room, and the light came from the small crevice below it. That door was *definitely* locked.

That was when he saw the horror in front of him.

A heart-shaped glass mold, filled to the brim with blood, labeled: *Nicholae, my love*.

His breath raced. Of course, she was insane. Of course, she was bloody and gory and Ez already knew this. But... this place was poisonous. What kind of woman keeps the blood of her dead husband? He had to get out; he had to! Ez shoved the dragon heir amulet, as well as some letters and a booklet from Miranda's desk into his satchel (for later research). But for now, he ran.

And slammed the door on that monster's lair.

Ez stood on the precipice of the abandoned sorcerer's tower, fear overtaking his senses. He wasn't stupid, but sensible wasn't an accurate description either. Ez's only real plan was to climb to the top of the sorcerer's tower and jump high enough for the clouds to hide him. He'd just fly from there. His vibrant vermillion scales wouldn't exactly blend in with the dark, two-in-the-morning sky, so he'd spray-painted his human form black.

And he looked like an idiot.

The world outside of his window was shivering cold. His hands reached for the icy steps, praying he wouldn't slip. The fall, well... thank the gods he was a Changeling. Every wrong grip and every little stumble could lead to a deadly drop. If he didn't make it high enough to get some cloud cover, he was a goner. Miranda wouldn't be happy that a fifty-foot dragon had made a guest appearance on the streets of Valaztein. As he approached the tower's top, the stones became smaller and icier. Just one more and—

No!

Ez gripped the tower with just the fingertips of his hand. A few seconds of incapacitating fear passed, and then he finally started moving. Only he was insane enough to climb a two-hundred-foot tower with so little care! Finally, he reached a stopping point. The view did not disappoint.

Wow.

Zurei was covered in frost. Icicles drooped from the rooftops of a dark city transformed into a world of glassy snow and shimmering stars. It was mystical. It was beautiful. It was hiding from a terrifying truth.

The truth of the night. The moment that dawn arrived, the frost no longer concealed palace secrets. Guards would strike and pummel civilians into obedience. Fathers would leave to work long hours in fields and factories. Mothers would scream for their children as they woke up and found them gone, taken by their queen of shadows.

They had no clue where, why, or who, but Ez did.

Not that any of it mattered now. His fears eased as the city faded into the next stone, the next step. This was just another operation, and disobeying the Queen was once again a normal thing. Gosh, the recklessness, the defiance! It reminded him of who he was.

Of who he had been.

The tower's peak gazed down at him, mere inches away. *Tip. Tap. Toe.*

Before he could analyze the footsteps, a black figure tackled him to the floor. They tumbled off the tower, fighting for breath. His senses became untrustworthy as he dangled upside down on the tower.

Oh, shoot.

After a quick glance, he caught his attacker's face. Ariah? She hung onto the inside of an open window, grasping his foot. Without breaking a sweat, she held both their weights with one hand.

Show-off.

"What the hell are you doing?" Ez demanded.

"Trying not to get us both killed."

"Well, you've been doing a pretty bad job of it lately."

"Do you even know what you're doing?" Ariah replied with an eye roll. "Guards are watching from every corner of this palace. Next time you should do the thrill-jumping in your room!" Huh? Then Ez looked up and instantly read her gaze. *Play along.*

"Fine. I'll go somewhere else." Ariah held in a sigh of relief. What was she doing?

"Come, idiot," she said and hoisted them both up. They rushed through the open window, glass shards shattering across the empty room. Ariah used the chaos to shove a crumpled piece of paper into his pocket. Then she left, slamming the door on her way out as if to complete the act.

Gosh, he would never understand her…

Ez paced towards his room and locked the bathroom door. *Free of Miranda's peering eyes.* He threw open the curtains and rushed into the shower, turning on the faucet. Ariah's handwriting was frantic and sloppy, but legible enough to get the message through.

Meet me at 5 near the river docks if you don't wanna die.

There were few things he desired less than that traitor's help, but it looked like he didn't have much of a choice.

Ariah waited at the mucky docks with that usual unreadable expression. Her black afro was wrapped in a blue Tashiki-style turban, indicating their destination. Ariah also obscured her face with a long cerulean scarf and giant aquamarine glasses.

"Are we being watched?" he mouthed. Ariah nodded a little too enthusiastically.

Clearly, they weren't actors.

"I need to throw something away," she said in a voice much higher than her own. "Will you come with me?" He nodded, attempting not to curl his hands into fists. He was going to kill her when this was over! What was her plan? How was he supposed to trust her after what she did?

It was like handing a sword to a murderer.

Actually, it *was* handing a sword to a murderer.

Ariah strolled to the dumpster behind them, and Ez trailed her. The moment they reached it, she kneeled as if to pick something. He mimicked her. Ariah smacked him hard and sent Ez plunging into the dumpster, the lid closing on him. Thank gosh, they cleaned the dumpster on Tuesday mornings! Only three items were in the dumpster: a curly red wig, almond-brown contact lenses, and a military uniform with the name tag "Tholin Merk" on it.

Ez quickly changed into the military uniform and attached the name tag. The wig and contact lenses were hard to get on, but he had done it plenty of times during missions. Especially the contacts because of his odd eye color. He slid out of the dumpster quickly, hoping no one would notice. Ariah had also changed into a military outfit.

"Come, let's go." She pointed to a military ship on the far side of the docks, and they strode towards it.

"Identification?" a guard asked as they tried to board the ship.

"Tholin Merk and Merissa Daily," Ariah replied.

"And what mission are you on?" the guard asked with a matching death stare.

"Well, that's an interesting question," Ez replied, hoping he didn't sound as shaky as he felt. "Because you *have* those records, don't you?"

"Umm... yes," the guard said, his suspicion fading away as he flipped through the pages of his list.

The tricks of a trained liar.

"No need for that," Ariah said in her new singsong voice. It was disgusting that it could make her sound like a person, not a monster.

The guard fumbled over his words as he let them pass.

"Have a good trip." As if that was gonna happen. Ez paced up the steel ramp, staring at the murky river water. It was a ruthless black, the color of a midnight sky. The Capital-Sun River connected Zurei to the Maruna Ocean and the palace to the rest of the world. *You're gonna find the heir,* he thought. Then a quieter, darker voice crept up into his heart. *You're gonna leave Naomi behind.*

Chapter 5: To Enter the Crossing - (Amethyst)

Kry, Tashiki

Amethyst always drowned when she entered a vision. Strangely, it was drowning only in appearance. Her lungs should've been gasping for air, her skin should've been freezing in the moonless water, and her eyes should've hurt from opening them.

But they didn't.

Because this wasn't real. Amethyst was only a spectator in whatever she was about to witness. As she lay in the murky water, a countdown began in her head. *How long will it take me to drown and wake up on land?* Fifteen, fourteen, thirteen… It was always fifteen seconds. Every. Single. Time.

The strange thing about her abilities was that they worked in two ways. First, she could manipulate time and turn back her clock to relive her timeline. Minutes, hours sometimes…

She'd once been able to go a day, but even that was by accident. There was so much to be explored within her powers. Could she travel to the future? If that was possible, could she screw things up permanently?

(You see, this is why parents exist. But apparently, hers weren't bothered to show up, so Amethyst was stuck with these dumb little powers.)

And the second way her powers worked: these weird visions. She could be perfectly fine, but three seconds later, her head was spinning and the world had gone black. The times they happened were just as unpredictable as the visions themselves.

Unlike when she backtracked time, her visions could be anywhere, anytime, through anyone's mind, and Amethyst couldn't interfere. Not even if she wanted to.

Once, she could control her powers. Now they controlled her.

But at least Grek would be there when she woke up. Grek would always be there. Because it was Grek.

Grek an alcoholic and a thief: the only ray of hope in that entire, run-down town.

Grek, the only person she had in the world who couldn't maintain a relationship other than hers.

Grek, who had been broken by his sister. And by the monsters who took her.

Only a few more seconds until she stopped drowning and reached a new visionscape (or whatever she should call these weird mini-realities). Six, five, four, three, two… Amethyst appeared on solid ground for a mere second, and suddenly she was falling. Again, none of it was new.

When she arrived, the sky of her visionscape wasn't really a sky, because it was orange and cracked, just like the ground should've been. That meant that the ground was a bluish-black color, and upside-down crows circled her feet. Their eyes were a deep forest green hue, but the inky crows missed their pupils. Suddenly, a wobbly wooden bridge pixelated below her.

Amethyst grasped the rope handles, feeling air instead of the reassurance that touch brought.

This was the Crossing.

The place where she had never reached the other side.

Amethyst awaited the slight thrust in the wind, the uncontrollable force that would shove her off the wobbly bridge before she could reach the end, but it didn't come. *Sooner or later I'll fall,* Amethyst reminded herself as she continued through the bridge. *Don't hold on to balance. I'm going to fall.* Three seconds later, she did, and the gut-wrenching feeling smacked her hard.

Amethyst knew that she wasn't falling into the sky. No pain could be felt in her visionscape, but that didn't make her mind register the terror as any less real.

The rocky floor she hit felt like nothing. It always did. The next part was the only thing that was different every time, so Amethyst paid close attention to her surroundings. An educated guess would've been that she was inside a cave, but that didn't make much sense. No, she was in some kind of manmade subterranean tunnel.

So, the same thing, but with fancier words and humans involved.

Which was made evident by a couple of things. The tunnels' edges were smooth and flawless, and several different openings looked anything but natural. Amethyst heard the faint whisper of voices and followed them, not caring to tip-toe. She rushed through the passageways, trusting only her ears to lead her to where she needed to go. Her eyes did her no good anyway because the only light came from a dim, blue fire lantern hung on one of the walls.

Finally, Amethyst came to a grand space in the labyrinth of tunnels, and she was staring at two figures, both draped in black robes. Amethyst focused on the most critical question: past or present?

The first voice continued to speak, hushed and quivering.

"Are you insane?" Hundreds of public presentations had made it very easy for Amethyst to decipher that voice. The dead king of Tashiki.

Yay! Everyone *loves* him.

Even the sarcasm in her brain annoyed her. However, she could draw a conclusion from the discovery of this dead king.

"Past it is," Amethyst muttered. But why would he be in an underground tunnel?

"Jiko, please!" the other figure (a man, she now realized) begged. Amethyst recognized the tone. She'd done it a lot when she was younger before she realized that stealing was much more effective. But who was begging in this vision? Searching for a light source, Amethyst set her eyes on another lantern hanging next to the second figure. Amethyst moved toward it, scouring for a face to go with that voice.

"Nik!" Jiko exclaimed, reprimanding the other figure for something. "We all have to do our part in protecting Anaji!" Anaji? Oh! Anaji was the dead queen, wasn't she? Killed in a time gap or whatnot?

What a poor, sad, unprecedented tragedy.
Yeah, right.

"You don't understand! Miri could wipe out an entire race! Jiko, you have to hide the dragon heir!" The man was yelling now, and Amethyst could feel him trembling. Miranda? The dragon heir? Wiping out a race?

"Look." King Jiko whispered so quietly Amethyst had to stop moving to hear him. "Anaji's harboring fugitives, people the Queen wants dead. If Miranda finds any proof of what she's doing, something like the dragon heir, she's as good as dead."

"I won't tell her. I promise." They both nodded. "It's the only way to keep her and the heir safe." Amethyst heard crying and realized that Nik was handing King Jiko a baby. Light flooded the room and the loud creak of a door opening followed. Amethyst relished the light because suddenly she could see everything very clearly.

The second figure pushed King Jiko and the baby, whom Amethyst guessed was the dragon heir, into a dark cavern and out of sight.

"Go," he whispered hurriedly. Amethyst now had a choice: follow the figure and find the "dragon heir" or discover the second figure's identity. Amethyst didn't move. The identity of the second figure was more intriguing at this moment and would probably be easier to follow.

Amethyst cursed, realizing that she wouldn't even be able to see the man *with* light because he was clothed in black and wore a mask. It was a dumb choice to stay, apparently. Two figures entered the room with Nik. One was the dead queen Anaji, and the other was also dressed in black, with only her emerald green eyes shimmering through the mask. (What was it with these people and masks?) Most importantly, the black figure was holding a knife to the late queen's throat, except the dagger was made of shadows.

"Let her go, Miri," Nik said. The black figure, Miri, didn't even lower the knife. "Let. Her. Go."

"I don't think I'd be making threats in your position, Niki," Miri replied.

"Go ahead. You might have some trouble explaining how a king and a queen died on the same day while you were watching."

"I can be very convincing." Amethyst saw Miri smirk inside her mask.

"What do you want? To kill me?"

"Why would I do that, Changeling?" Her eyes darkened at the word. "I love you, Niki. I always have." That made no sense. None whatsoever, so why would she say it? Amethyst's head was spinning in circles now, not just because of the shock from the vision. The man curled his fists and muttered something Amethyst couldn't hear.

Suddenly, the entire scene exploded as the night was stolen by fire and shadows.

Chapter 6: Heather Queen - (Naomi)

```
Dopül, Valaztein
```

Naomi ran towards the stream. The murky river water rushed over her body like a roaring fall. Her burns screamed. Her bruises yelled. Her cuts howled. Naomi threw herself at the water, feeling relief as her skin touched the dark liquid. It was like jumping into the moat, minus the soul-crushing fear. Miko scurried away from Naomi's splashes, disgusted by the dirty, polluted, probably freezing water.

Loud voices boomed in the distance. *Shoot, guards!* She pointed to a tree.

"Go!" she mouthed to Miko as the guards entered the clearing. She submerged herself in the water, holding a long, deep breath.

Geesh! That's cold!

She had to calm down; there were more important things.

Then a darker question hit her. Why weren't the bounty hunters on her trail too? Maybe the Queen had made up some story? Perhaps she needed to make the people believe something that brainwashing couldn't?

Her breath was running out, and the guards didn't appear to be leaving. What was happening? All she heard was thunderous stomping before everything went silent. Naomi slowly came up, resisting the urge to gasp for air. She waited for Miko's fluffy tail to peek out of the trees, but it didn't.

Miko was the distraction.

Naomi sprinted through the trees, willing her frail legs to carry her.

"Not Miko," Naomi whispered to herself. "I can't lose him too." There were no words to describe her relief when she found Miko, chased by three guards, but surpassing them at an incredible speed as he flew through the thick evergreen foliage. The guards had their backs to her, and they had unknowingly passed her the upper hand.

Naomi still didn't have the energy to use her powers, and there was no point in making them pass out just to mimic the action herself. She motioned for Miko to break a branch and throw it at her because she couldn't risk them hearing her. Miko did just that, and she let the branch hit the ground, but then silently picked it up. Miko had stopped, giving Naomi the perfect lack of motion from the guards that she needed.

Naomi kicked the first guard in a soft spot on the back of his knee that Ariah had shown her during training long ago. That sent him stumbling forward, the other guard with him. Just in case, Naomi stabbed the second guard in the eye with her stick and followed this process for the other guard. Once they were all in a heap on the floor, Miko leaped onto her arm, and they both sprinted through the frozen forest.

Her breath was heavy; Naomi could see it in the cold air as she ran through the snowy forest. The tall, frosted evergreens sheltered them from unwanted eyes. Only Miranda's army would be crazy enough to go out in this weather anyway. Like all the other furry little creatures that hopped around the lofty trees, Miko relished the weather.

Naomi, on the other hand… It felt like her blood was frozen.

There were more than fifteen encounters with the Queen's minions that day. If the Queen wasn't going to stop, Naomi couldn't afford to either. She raced straight through the night, unsure of her destination. But it was far, far away from this hell.

In between the thick foliage, Naomi spotted a flicker of light.

"A guard tower," she whispered. A map! Warmth! Maybe even food? It was all overwhelming. Naomi rushed up the stairs and picked open the lock. The faint moonlight was not very helpful in this endeavor.

Ez was clearly a better lock-picker than she was.

No. Naomi refused to think of him.

Liar.

Monster.

Traitor.

She dashed up the spiral staircase and knocked out the two people watching before they could report anything through their odd little devices.

A green model stood before her. Not a hypnotization map… No, this was something different.

A colonization map, Naomi realized. The Queen placed flags everywhere where she had established control. Naomi spotted a small red spot, free from the Queen's reign. Naomi's safe haven: The Elemento Tribe Territories.

Naomi found red ink on the table and wrote her to-do list on her wrist.

Kill Ariah

Dethrone the Queen

Naomi hesitated before writing the next part. This was for her country. This was for her people. But that tiny voice in her head whispered a callous truth. You want this because he hurt you. Because he smashed your heart like glass. And he didn't care. She wouldn't have spent two years in hell if he did. Her people wouldn't be colonized by Miranda if he did. Her country wouldn't be scattered if he did. She wouldn't be broken if he did. So Naomi carved the final task of her to-do list on her hand.

Kill Ez

```
Doomsday Cliffs of the Elemento Tribe Territories,
Valaztein
```

When she reached the jagged mountains of the ever-terrifying Doomsday Cliffs, wrenching guilt climbed up her spine. Just her presence here endangered hundreds of lives. Miranda's guards could be on her trail any minute! Still, what was the alternative? Let the Queen have her? Let that murderer win?

Firo would be coming through the giant wall of flames any moment, so Naomi had to think swiftly. Would seeking refuge with the tribes be an act of cowardice or bravery? Would she be hiding, or waiting for the moment to fight? Was there a difference?

Naomi's legs quivered beneath her, threatening to buckle. *Breathe.* But she couldn't. Not when the fate of a kingdom was in her next breath. Every choice, every second she spent near this perilous mountain... had a consequence.

Finally, it came. Breath came like a vicious current bashing through the boulders of a river. And yet, there wasn't enough air in the world to distract her from the choice at hand. If she walked to those cliffs, the Queen would surely come after her and kill the people of the Elemento Tribe Territories. If she didn't, she'd kill them anyway. Every choice was dangerous, but making none was even worse.

Then, a crevice unfurled in the wall of flames, revealing two stone-faced Firo. Neither of them was Chief Vorum, but they would do. Before she could mutter her name, the wind warped around her. A dagger flew towards her from the far-off woods, leaving her no time to gasp. The last thing she saw before everything went black was the blade of the dagger, coated in scarlet and sinking into her shoulder.

When she woke, the mountain's hazy mist of clouds emerged around her. Naomi reached out to touch the fluffy clouds, motivated by fatigue and delirium. As her arm shifted, a burning pain rushed through her shoulder. That put everything into perspective.

There was a knife pierced into her body. The Firo protected her. They were climbing up the cliffs. Her pursuer climbed slowly but clearly had the aim to substitute for it. She should be dead. She wasn't.

"Climb!" the man who was carrying her shouted.

"What do you think I'm doing?" hollered a voice below her. Naomi slumped back into the man's grip.

"I'm out of ammo!" the second man shouted from below. Oh, their pursuers weren't only shooting, they were climbing too.

Great.

A flying object struck the second man's ear, and he let out a quick shriek. They needed ammo. But where? That's when insanity truly consumed her. Naomi yanked the dagger from her shoulder and thrust it at their attacker.

The figure slipped off the side of the mountain, clinging to a flimsy branch. How could she just watch that person fight for their life?

What a horrible way to die. Naomi thought. *Knowing there's nothing you could do.* She had to make a choice. Save the person who was trying to kill her, or let the guilt kill her anyway.

No one should have that choice. No one should choose who lives and who dies.

"Save them," Naomi whispered to the man who was carrying her, hoping it was loud enough. The man nodded, and Naomi attempted to smile.

"Aiko, save the person!"

"You want me to save the guy who's trying to kill us?" the other man demanded.

"Yes. Before he plummets to his death, please." The two men separated. A few minutes later, Naomi reached the top. Gratitude rushed through her as she was propped onto a rolling bed.

Hundreds of Firo rushed towards her from across the rocky plateau, trying to catch a glimpse of her. They probably thought that

Naomi was a miracle; the dead princess, finally coming to rescue them. Oh, she prayed that she could.

Medics pushed the hordes of people away, rushing her across the craggy terrain and to an enormous building situated right beside Chief Vorum's house. Ah, finally: a hospital. The rest of her trip was quite blurry. Slamming doors, faded faces… There was a room with bleary blue lights flashing in her eyes where a man bandaged her shoulder. After that, she was hooked up to steaming machines.

Clearly, the Firo had no access to MagikThesia 'cause every second a new wave of pain arrived in her shoulder.

The next days went by in a haze. Shoulder meds, movement training, and bandaging were all a jumbled mess of memories. The only thing she was at risk to die of soon was boredom. Despite her several requests to be let out of the hospital, the Firo didn't seem to take a hint.

One day, a rather grumpy nurse walked into her room, annoyed with Naomi's reluctance. "See if you can do five pushups with that busted shoulder, and I will personally see to it that you are discharged."

So she did. It hurt like hell, but they finally let her leave the hospital.

Miko crept onto her shoulder as Naomi left the massive stone building far behind her. She searched for someone who might know where the chief would be at 1:30 P.M., and right on the marble footsteps of his mansion, an answer awaited her.

"Take me to the chief," Naomi told the nearest guardsman. He nodded. Naomi followed him through the dark alleyways of his mansion, taking in every stone and detail. Whoa, it was quite a sight to behold. Iron details decorated the fortress-like steel walls. Jagged stone pillars touched the lofty ceilings, carved with gems and silver.

Despite its massiveness, guardsmen stood at every corner of Chief Vorum's estate. They really were waiting for Miranda.

Miranda. That brought her back to another thing. What had happened to her relentless pursuer while she had been climbing the cliffs? Was this person working for Miranda?

Finally, Naomi reached a familiar room, the weaponry. The thousands of elaborate bronze weapons still kept her in awe. The shelves held all kinds of lethal beauties, which remained wrapped in metal and magic. Chief Vorum, surrounded by five equally muscular men, stood behind a display of bronze spears.

"I thought you were dead," he said plainly. Naomi had learned the hard way that the Firo weren't very keen on introductions or greetings. "That is what Queen Miranda said, and I wouldn't put it past her."

"I am well alive, thanks to you and your people." Miko grinned from his perch on her shoulder.

"It is our duty to protect our queen."

Naomi was taken aback. "I am no queen."

"I am afraid that that, my Queen, is *your* duty."

"What happened to the person one of the guards saved?" Naomi asked, curious and desperate to change the subject. Before she could worry about becoming a queen, she'd have to dethrone the existing one.

"Oh, the girl," Chief Vorum responded. "She's in that cell over there. You can speak to her if you like. I must warn you, though, her trial's in a few hours and she hasn't been very responsive to reasoning."

Naomi nodded. "Thank you." He took that as a cue to leave, and Naomi paced over to the cell where they were holding "the girl." Huh, it was the same cell in which she had been held the first time. She never thought she'd be so glad to see her own prison cell.

Déjà vu.

"Hello?" Naomi asked as she opened the door. "Is anyone there?"

"Just me," a voice responded.

Naomi was determined not to act startled.

"It's rather dark," she said. "Is it alright if I turn on the lights?"

"Whatever."

Naomi flipped the small switch and stared at the figure facing her. She had curly waist-length hair, the color of velvet dipped in crimson dye. Her lips were a natural scarlet, redder than a blood moon. Dark brown eyes shot a stare at Naomi like daggers, cold and unreadable. And the most shocking thing, she couldn't be older than fourteen.

A kid.

"What's your name?" The girl took a few seconds to roll her eyes before responding.

"Heather Queen, you?"

"Naomi Elistaire."

"Like, the crazy princess? Aren't you supposed to be dead?"

"Supposedly." Naomi sighed. Her face begged Heather to say something, but the girl didn't seem like she wanted to budge. After a couple of minutes, Naomi couldn't stand the silence.

"What are you, fifteen? You're pretty young to be working for the Queen."

"Fourteen." Heather leaned back into her cell wall. "What's with the monkey?"

"Who? Miko?" Naomi looked back at her shoulder, realizing that Miko might actually be an odd sight for most. "He's an old friend."

"Do you people have chairs around here?" Heather complained, finally standing up. Naomi quickly viewed one thing. Heather was very, very thin. Naomi decided against asking why. Experience had taught her that small things like that could have horrible, twisted backstories.

Especially if this girl had any connection to Miranda.

"I'd get you one, but I'm not sure the Firo would like it."

"Oh, well," Heather said. "Either way, I don't think they're too big on the 'one final meal' thing here."

"One final meal?"

"Yeah, you know, before they execute me?"

"What?" Naomi exclaimed. "They're not gonna kill you!"

"Then what?" Heather interrogated. "Torture me? Break me? Use me? Trade me back to the Queen? Like she'd even want me." Her words were coated with a thick layer of sarcasm.

"What is wrong with you?" Naomi blurted out the words, even surprising herself at saying them. Heather laughed, a long, teenage laugh. A laugh that should be used after a friend tells a joke at a party. What a horrible placement of it. Heather stared her straight in the eyes. What were they filled with? Sorrow or tears? Guilt or blame? The only thing they gave away was the crazed coating of glossy derangement that hid everything.

"Oh, Elistaire, you have no idea."

A few hours later, Heather's trial came. Jitters crept up Naomi's arms. Why? Wasn't this the girl who attempted to *kill* her a few days ago? Naomi was saving another life; that's all that mattered.

BANG!

The wooden mallet slammed against a silver gong, signaling the start of the trial. Crimson flames circled Heather, engulfing what now seemed to be her fragile figure. A man stood on an iron platform, his eyes reflecting the red tint of the flames. The room was searing, the trial intense. And then there was Heather, seated amidst the flames, her slim body barely filling up half the chair. Despite her petite frame and minimal age, Heather looked anything but innocent.

Miko hooted beside Naomi with that unforgiving face. Apparently, the snow monkey could hold a grudge for longer than Naomi could.

"The defendant is accused of the following crimes: armed assault with knives, several murder attempts…"

The list went on, but Naomi ignored it. Instead, she zoned out to a pleasant dreamland. Sometime through her cloudy hallucination, Naomi realized that all those pills probably hadn't worn off yet.

Finally, the interrogation began.

"What is your name?" the man asked, his face gloomy due to the firelights on Heather.

"Heather Queen."

"Do you confess to the list of crimes in front of you?" Heather burst into tears.

"I'm sorry!" she cried. "I didn't want to hurt Naomi. She was so sweet and, and…"

The interrogator softened and asked, "Can you explain what happened?"

"Okay." Heather nodded and wiped the tears from her face, though they kept coming. "I was a maid in the palace." She looked down, sobbing at the memory.

"Can you calm down, please?" the interrogator asked.

"Yes, sorry," Heather mumbled. "Then, then… She took me and tortured me. It was like voodoo magic, but I was so scared. I thought she was going to kill me… Instead, she just spelled me. I blacked out after that, but I think she wanted me as her puppet."

"You must now present at least five valuable pieces of evidence to solidify your… outlandish claims."

"Okay," Heather mumbled. "Um… What kind of evidence?"

"Do you have any scars of the Queen's torture?"

"Yes." Heather dragged up her sleeve, revealing a deep gash that stretched from her shoulder to her forearm. *Oh, memories.*

"Evidence verified," said the interrogator. "Anything more?"

"Yes," Heather replied. "I need Elistaire to confirm this evidence."

"Elistaire?" asked the interrogator.

"Oh, right," Heather replied, plastering on a sweet smile. "Princess Naomi."

"Princess Naomi, will you testify in the court of the Firo?"

Miko gaped at her. *No way you're gonna help out this girl. She's playing you. She tried to kill you!*

"Sure." Despite her own logic, Naomi paced down to the ring. All the meanwhile, Miko bit her shoulder and rolled his eyes. The ring of fire lowered, and Naomi strutted through.

"The Queen's eyes turn black when she uses her powers, right?" Heather asked.

"Yes," Naomi responded, half suspicious, half stunned. How would she know that?

"You have similar powers," the interrogator said. "Would you care to demonstrate?"

"No." Naomi walked out of the ring of fire and back to her seat, ignoring everyone still staring at her. Empathy ended where her own torture began. Naomi wouldn't act as her mother or play the witch. Because she wasn't. No matter what they believed.

"Shall we proceed?"

Heather let another round of tears escape her, which caused another wave of pity from the crowd.

"Yes." Heather slipped an object out of her pocket. "This was the washcloth that I used to clean the stable doors." Sure enough, the dirty white fabric had the palace symbol embedded in it. The interrogator stared at it for a couple of minutes before responding.

"Evidence will be taken in for further investigation." Naomi hadn't the slightest clue why. Every palace employee symbol was hand-woven and impossible to replicate.

Heather then presented an apron and a horse brush, which were both "taken in for further investigation." After two hours of watching them administer DNA potions and trace fingerprint marks with a special Firo technique, Naomi was about done with the trial.

"None of our standard procedures have come to contradict the defendant's claims." Heather sighed, and the tears that had streamed across her face for two hours halted. Then, the chief walked into the ring of fire and hushed the interrogator.

"Three lives were almost taken. In accordance with our ancient rules, it is only fair that these three lives get to decide the fate of the person who tried to take their life away from them. If two or more of these people agree to a pardon, Heather Queen shall be saved. If not, you will all be witnessing an execution three days from now."

"Please step up into the ring of fire." A man stood up from his seat and moved towards the ring of fire. Naomi tensed. This wasn't the man who had carried her, but he had saved Heather's life. She just had to hope he had the heart to do it again.

"Do you, Derek Mar, grant Heather Queen a pardon?" the chief asked

"Yes." Derek stepped out of the fire.

"Gongram Mar, please step into the ring of fire," Cherif boomed. To the Firo, Cherif was a goddess, her powerful voice looming over their every decision. Her words, well... they were more binding than any law. Sure enough, the man who had carried her walked into the fire.

"Do you, Gongram Mar, grant Heather Queen a pardon?"

"No." Gongram stepped away from the fire. Then, her name was called, and Naomi once again stepped into the middle of the room.

"Do you, Naomi Elistaire, grant Heather Queen a pardon?" Miko shook his head at her as if pleading with Naomi to say no. He hooted, and Naomi was surprised when she could understand him perfectly.

This person tried to kill you. She's probably working with Miranda.

But Miko was wrong.

No one else dies.

Not unless they have to.

"Yes."

The crowd yelled in agreement and the chief stepped out of the fire. As he left, the ring of fire flickered out.

"Heather Queen has been proclaimed innocent! The trial is closed." Even the chief grinned as he stepped off his platform, so Naomi allowed herself a smile too.

A few hours later, Heather arrived at her cell to gather her things, aka a pack of gum.

There, Naomi waited.

"Congratulations," she said.

"On what? Good acting?"

Naomi gasped.

"Was any of that true?" Heather sighed and wiped off her sad puppy dog face as if she was relieved to stop lying. Then Heather grinned and popped a bubble with her gum.

"Not a single word."

Naomi was woken by shadows everywhere. Her fear drowned out the screams of agony from the people in nearby doors. No, no, no, no... how could this be happening? All she could think was run; run away from the shadows. Run away from the darkness. She didn't change out of her nightgown, not caring if people gasped at the abundant collections of scars covering her body.

Run. Run, run, run far away from the shadows. Her palms were sweaty and her eyes bulged, but suddenly, she understood. Everyone craved the light, but she only craved it to escape the darkness. But never could she escape the darkness. She could not escape the darkness because she was it; she created it. And no one can run from themselves, not without destroying them and everyone they love in the process.

Run.

Then there was nothing. Except the screams and the fear and the tears and the sweat and the black. Except for the darkness. Shadows were everywhere, and faces were nowhere. The only faces that she saw were her mother's, and then her own, equally reflected in the darkness. Her whole life's algorithm was reduced to that of a frightened animal:

Run. Hide. Survive.

But she couldn't even do that, because she stopped running and collapsed on the floor. After all, why would she be running from herself? That seemed wrong, though. It had to be, because the only logical first step in her algorithm was to run, but her legs wouldn't run. Hiding was hopeless because movement would be required for that.

Shadows trapped her. They choked her.

No one could know that she was broken. That was what she had told herself, wasn't it? But everyone knew that she was broken.

Now they all knew that she was terrified and broken and oh, so alone.

Then there was a hand, and it was small, but in her mind, it was three times bigger. It was her father's. And he was holding her and they were both in the light. In reality, she wasn't in the light yet, but she was being taken away from the darkness at least. So, she watched as her father's hand, Heather's hand in reality, took her away from the darkness, and into the after light of her own fear.

Naomi and Heather stood crouching inside the Doomsday Cliffs. Clearly, the Firo had never really trusted their country's rulers. Instead, they had built the secret bunkers that Naomi and Heather were hiding in, which were practically impenetrable. The bunkers were, quite simply, *inside* the mountain. The Queen had attempted to get through the wall several times since Naomi was imprisoned, but this had been the first that succeeded. At least, that's what the gossipy man next to her had said.

"So, that was real?"

"Yep," Heather responded, popping a gum bubble. "Real as the sky, Elistaire." Naomi didn't know what to say. Words could not express her gratitude.

"Thank you." It wasn't enough for Heather to understand, though. Naomi knew that.

"Whatever. You're actually pretty cool. Didn't know you were so psychotic, though," Heather said.

"You won't tell anyone, will you?"

Heather looked annoyed to have to stop chewing her gum. "Course not."

Naomi sighed. "Thank you."

Heather rolled her eyes. "You're strange. And also, does this mean we're even? Like, I tried to kill you. You saved my life. I saved your life. I won't rat you out."

"I guess," Naomi said, and Heather grinned.

"Nice."

"What's 'nice'?" Naomi asked. What Heather said next surprised her.

"I'm meeting the seventeen-year-old rebel princess who's trying to kill her own mother. That's what's nice."

Naomi squinted, not sure what to say. "Thank you?"

"No problem. Can I chew my gum now?" Naomi laughed, the terror slowly crumbling away.

"Please return to your normal dorms and homes," boomed a voice from the walls. Cherif, again. The entire room burst into quiet cheers and suppressed sighs. No one knew what came next. Then, all at once, the shuffling of feet enveloped everything, and Naomi rushed out of the bunker with them, joy coloring her face.

Naomi was stopped before she could reach her quarters, though, because a figure walked through the crowd, everyone making way for him to get through.

"The chief," Heather muttered. The Firo did not waste time, so whatever Chief Vorum had come to say had to be important.

"As you all know, Miranda Elistaire is, well..." Naomi was surprised by the ease he said the words, as if her mother was not a queen at all.

"Not Elistaire," Naomi shouted from the crowd. "That's my father's name." Chief Vorum looked surprised, but somehow not angry.

"Miranda, then," Chief Vorum repeated, "has made several attempts to pass our walls, and only this one has succeeded. Three Firo lives were lost in this attempt, all protecting Queen Naomi. A meeting will be called immediately between the tribe leaders and Queen Naomi. Thank you."

Naomi resisted the urge to scream. Three lives lost. Because of *her*, because she was too inept to stop it. Because she had crumbled on the floor, while brave soldiers were risking their lives for her. How could these people call her their queen? She could barely protect herself, much less thousands of people.

"It's not your fault," Heather said. "They know it's not." The words meant nothing to her, and she suddenly wished that she was back in the dragon base, protected and rebellious. Of course, things couldn't be so simple anymore, no matter what she dreamed of.

Then Naomi was snapped back to reality by Chief Vorum's gruff voice.

"Queen Naomi, please report to the Border."

The Border was no joke. It literally stood at the meeting point between land and sky. The council assembly was held at the foot of the Doomsday Cliffs, where a hill stood to hold the king of the Earthie, who kneeled on the natural turf, his grassy robes draped across the greenery.

Despite his tranquilizing appearance, the earth king's expression was grim, solemn, and extremely worrying to Naomi.

The beru of the Airam and his granddaughter sat with their legs crossed on a couple of clouds. They wore cerulean cloaks, and marble necklaces hung over their necks, decorating their rather simple attire with beads and symbols. Written in ink all over their blue capes were prayers. The Airam liked to write down their prayers on their garments, and they prayed more frequently as difficult times approached. Naomi had seen this happening before the battle with Miranda two years ago, but she had never seen their robes as crowded as this. They could barely fit another word in! Clearly, something was wrong.

The only remotely calming figure was the queen of the sea. A small saltwater spring the color of her name made a perfect seat for Queen Aquamarine. Her entire body was completely submerged in water, except for her shell-based braided hairdo, and her delicate, sugar-like face. Miko leaped towards Queen Aquamarine, the first queen he had ever met.

Naomi thought of telling him that there was no way that she was going to let him onto her shoulder now that his adventures to greet Queen Aquamarine had rendered him soaking wet, but thought better of it, considering the circumstances. She sat down in one of the Firo's metal chairs and listened closely to the meeting.

"Welcome," said Queen Aquamarine. "Now, we—"

"There's no time for formality, Aquamarine," Chief Vorum interrupted. "The decision must be made in a matter of hours."

"What decision?" Naomi asked.

The room went quiet.

"Miranda has penetrated our walls," the king of the Earthie explained. "Only the Firo's defenses remain."

"Are the people alright?" she blurted out. How could this be happening?

"Yes," said Queen Aquamarine. "They are all transitioning to the Doomsday Cliffs as we speak." Naomi let out a much-needed breath.

"How many casualties?" Naomi couldn't stop herself from asking.

"Fifty-three."

"Now," Chief Vorum interrupted. "You have a decision to make, Naomi."

"What decision?"

"Miranda might spare us if we give in to her, but if we try to escape—" the leader of the Airam said, and Queen Aquamarine finished his sentence.

"It could be a massacre."

"If you stay here, it *will* be a massacre," Naomi said, annoyed by their ignorance. "She's not going to let you survive after you've defied her for so long. She isn't forgiving. Miranda knows as well as I do that if she lets you live and the people find out about it, she could lose control. Please, trust me, I know."

"Where would we go?" the beru of the Airam asked.

"I don't know. Tashiki? Lightmoon?"

"Tashiki would be better," said Chief Vorum. "Their government's in pieces and they're in the middle of a coronation process for the orphaned prince. Their immigration system is hardly what it was before. Besides, the government wouldn't really be playing a grand part in an escapade like this."

"Alright."

"How are you suggesting we escape?" Queen Aquamarine asked Naomi.

"Underwater. Below the ocean floor. The Earthie could make the tunnels, and the Oceani could make sure we all breathe," Naomi replied.

"And if a ship comes?" the beru of the Airam questioned.

"The Airam could go up every once and a while to scout for ships."

"Understood," Chief Vorum said. "Does anyone have an objection to this plan?"

The beru's granddaughter spoke next. "I understand that survival is currently our only initiative, but I'd like to know the long-term benefits of this plan regarding the rebellion."

The room went quiet once more. What was Naomi supposed to answer to that? How could they worry about the rebellion while they barely had days before all of their lives were ended? Wait... something she had said could work.

"An orphaned prince?" Naomi finally asked. "Prince Urumi?"

The king of the Earthie covered his mouth, shocked. "You haven't heard?"

Naomi sighed, shaking her head. Wow, she had missed so many things while she was in the Crown Maze. Uh, that face the earth king made... It meant: *Oh, right. She was tortured for a really long time by the queen and missed the last two years. Poor girl.* Frankly, it was annoying, but Queen Aquamarine ended Naomi's misery and gave her an answer.

"King Jiko died a few weeks ago, darling. Prince Urumi's coronation is in less than thirty days."

Naomi grinned. Not at King Jiko's death, though; she wasn't a maniac. No matter how horrible a king he was diplomatically, she wouldn't be happy about his death. No, she grinned, because a tiny sliver of opportunity had just opened up for her, and the moment that the prince had his coronation, it would close.

Through many years of living the pure royal life, Naomi had learned all about the strange things that were interims. Before another ruler takes the throne, the kingdom is at its very weakest, and is ready to be molded into the next reign. Additionally, it was the only time that the ruler-to-be could possibly be found without a full cabinet of advisors. If Naomi could find Prince Urumi at that time, and convince him to support the rebellion, Tashiki could be the rebellion's first international ally.

"Moving to Tashiki will also bring us closer to our long-term goals, because the prince's way of thinking could be different from his father's. If we present him with a proposition to help the rebellion, we could find an ally with Tashiki," Naomi said.

"We will set out at dawn tomorrow, then," Queen Aquamarine finalized. "Before Miranda can strike again." Several nods of agreement followed, but Naomi still had one more question.

It had been shooting arrows at her heart since the moment that it had been announced, and Naomi couldn't help but have it on her conscience.

"Those guards," she choked as she said the words. "The ones that saved me. Why would they protect me?"

"They weren't protecting you," Chief Vorum said. "They were protecting the rebellion." Naomi gave him a puzzled look, but her answer came from behind her.

"Oh darling, don't you know?" Queen Aquamarine said. "You are the rebellion. If not a leader... than a martyr."

Chapter 7: Losing Air Supply - (Naomi)

```
The Corussant Sea, Tashiki, And Valaztein Border
```

Naomi's lungs longed for air, but instead, they were only given the vague illusion of it from the system that the Oceani were using to keep her alive. She reminded herself that no matter how sick and tired she was of the wretched sea, it was the safest way to Tashiki.

Safe. The word felt sarcastic, as if she was mocking herself.

Heather seemed to be having similar thoughts about the sea, though, because she looked ready to puke. By the time Naomi realized that she had been staring at Heather for a while, the fourteen-year-old girl had already given her the death stare.

"What?" Heather replied. "I've got sea sickness."

A pang of pity shot through Naomi. Chances were that the pressure, starvation, stress, and dehydration didn't help much either. Naomi guided her thoughts away from Heather's personal problems. If Naomi didn't stop meddling in other people's problems, she was going to end up dead. It was better to focus on her situation in the present and get through one thing at a time. Currently, she was stuck right in the middle of the commotion of terrified Firo, so there was barely enough space to see the actual ocean.

They swam through an underwater tunnel created by the Oceani. On either side, hundreds of tons of swirling navy water were being kept at bay by their aquatic friends. Without them... the pressure alone (not to mention the no air part) would leave them crushed.

A loud hoot resonated from her shoulder, and Naomi momentarily felt jealous of Miko. He looked perfectly comfortable in his magic Oceani air bubble. Meanwhile, she and Heather were getting dizzy just swimming. How was that fair?

Naomi resisted the urge to ask how much time was left, even though time, a basic characteristic in human life, was so often taken away from her. Like in the Crown Maze. Like in that dark, cold, terrifying place that was meant to torture her into insanity. And now, she wondered whether it had.

That was when the walls started closing in on her. She couldn't breathe. *This isn't real. This isn't real,* she reminded herself. But it felt like it. It felt like Miranda was right next to her, and the world was spinning in circles, and Ez was holding a knife to her back, and Ariah was murdering Infitri and—

No.

Breathe. Relax.

The tunnel returned to normal, and Naomi stood there, breathing heavily, but breathing nonetheless.

Then, a faint beeping sound resonated in the distance, growing louder and louder until it was audible to everyone she could see. Most of them covered their ears, but Naomi didn't bother, too busy listening to care. The sound was like a fading memory, so familiar, yet impossible to comprehend. From her millions of classes at the palace, Naomi finally remembered that it was some kind of magical system, most likely from a ship. Already, that wasn't good news, but the last beep in a sequence sent everything spiraling back to her.

The beeping was from one of her mother's body heat radiation systems.

The system was only available for Valazteinian military ships.

The ship must have come to prevent an escape attempt from Naomi, and now it had found one.

And lastly, there was no way for anyone else to know what it was.

"Heather!" Naomi yelled over all the commotion. "You need to get me to the nearest tribe leader."

Heather turned around and uncapped her ears. "What?"

"That radiation system is from one of Miranda's military ship body heat radiation systems," Naomi explained.

Heather blinked. "From *what*, you said?"

"The Queen knows where we are and now we're being tracked by a ship of her military."

"Great," Heather deadpanned, continuing to chew her gum.

"Seriously, we have to get to a tribe leader!"

"There's no time. The nearest tribe leader's at least six hundred people away." Naomi scanned around her, searching for something, anything, that could help them.

"Wait!" Naomi's head spun around to the nearest wall of water. "I've got an idea." Naomi grabbed the nearest Oceani citizen, who wasn't hard to find because they were scattered all over the place to keep people breathing. Annoyingly, the man didn't budge, so Miko, who was currently still relaxing on her shoulder, bit him.

Though she would have preferred to know that Miko was safe in the little tunnel, Naomi took the chance that she had. The man's momentary lapse in concentration opened a crack in the wall, and Naomi swiftly swam through it, Miko clinging to her arm.

She quickly became aware of an overarching obstacle as she swam outside the magic-made water tunnel: there was no air supply out here. And the pressure... every bone in her body was ready to break, and Miko wasn't looking too hot either. Not helping the matter was the undeniable fact that she still had a few minutes to go before she could reach the surface. So, she made a little bubble of her own (made of shadow, of course). Sure, it didn't help much with the breathing, but at least her bones didn't feel like bricks anymore.

Her only hope was to just keep swimming. Up, up, up, up. Though now liberated from their painful compression, her lungs ached for air. Finally, she saw a dim light and swam even faster, throwing Miko up for air before she came up herself.

Air. What a wonderful, wonderful thing. She would've stayed there forever, relishing the sweet morning air, but of course, that couldn't last long. Naomi saw the military boat coming near her, a steel monstrosity in the water, its engines coughing up smoke. She swam to catch it! Her fingers were already withered from all the water, but she grasped one of the windows of the lower cabins, refusing to let go. She thrashed at it with her hand, but once it became clear that it was impossible to break it, Naomi was faced with only one choice. Again, she had to use her most hated weapon: her powers.

Because they sucked the energy out of her.

Because they transformed her into a monster.

Because they reminded her of just how easily she could become her mother.

It was a quick process, nothing too difficult, but equally draining on her energy. The shadows that leaped from her hands broke the window in a matter of seconds, and they were free to enter. Once she and Miko had crammed through the opening, Naomi analyzed her surroundings. She stood in a small dorm room with two sets of bunk beds and a large map of the boat on a wall. The radiation control room was only three rooms away. Perfect! Once she disabled the radiation system, she could jump back to the tunnel and continue on with the escape.

"Miko, go out and make sure the hallway is clear," Naomi said.

The snow monkey did as he was told, and once she received a thumbs-up, Naomi slid right into the radiation control room.

The room was originally white, but because it was lit by a bluish hue, it had an aquamarine color to it. The room looked very techy, but Naomi now realized it wasn't.

Because at the front of the control panel was a manual that read: "Terrosystem: A Guide to Black Magic and Energy." Naomi shuffled through it like an animal chasing its prey.

The first page read: "The Terrosystem is an incredibly powerful energy system designed by the monarchs of Valaztein to further the kingdom technologically. Using Black magic energy, all advanced devices and systems that are exclusive to Valaztein are powered. The energy source from which this Black magic energy is taken is still unknown."

Unknown to the average person, maybe, but Naomi knew exactly where Black magic energy comes from. People. Innocent, cruelly treated people. She swore to herself: *I will find them, and I will save them.*

Because this was insanity. Every electronic she had ever known, from EzmoPads to voice amplifiers, were all part of a delicate system the Queen had made. And at the root of this system was the ever-growing power of Black magic.

That was enough. She had to return to the original reason she was in that room. Naomi shoved the manual into her bag and continued inspecting the room. Soon afterward, Naomi noticed the hundreds of panels, buttons, switches, and levers that covered the walls, and she faltered. How was she going to disable anything in this disaster?

A groaning sound resonated from a chair to her far right, and she quickly knocked out the man in the chair before he could cause any trouble. Naomi lifted the man from the odd position he had landed in, which revealed a whole array of levers and buttons. Gosh, how was she ever gonna find the right one? And then Miko jumped from her shoulder and started dancing on the switchboard, pressing everything. Literally every button, switch, and lever.

"Miko!" Naomi screamed as every light in the room turned red and messages shot up like bullets on the screen.

Then, a little message popped up: *RADIATION SYSTEM DISABLED. Would you like to erase all recent data?*

Naomi selected "yes" on the screen, giddy with relief. Three seconds later, alarms started blaring.

Naomi rushed up a random staircase on the boat, well aware that at least twenty guards were following her. Miko was still resting on her shoulders, but he looked like he was about to leap off and bite someone. Her legs were burning, but finally, *finally*, she reached the top floor of the boat. Smoke gushed out of the engines behind her, and the waves crashed against faraway boulders. The moonless sky was a gloomy sapphire blue, with no stars to interrupt the darkness.

It was as if the stars hadn't deemed the night important enough to show.

In that moment of chaotic panic, Naomi froze. Soldiers came at her from every side until she was cornered at the edge of the ship. If she slipped, Naomi was staring at a pretty terrible landing in the merciless water, which seemed to be revealing a new boulder every few seconds.

Suddenly, a speck of flaming red appeared from the top of the mainsail. A girl was swinging on a rope, her curly red hair the only speck of color in the darkness. Heather. On her way to where Naomi was standing, she knocked out at least five soldiers, and that filled Naomi with a fiery hope. So, she also started to fight the guards nearest to her.

One guard. Two. Three. Wow! She had gotten much better at this.

Wait...

Somehow, Naomi made out a traitorous face in all the commotion—Ariah's face. Naomi stumbled back and left a spot open where someone managed to punch her ribs. Despite her incredible skill at combat, Heather also seemed to be having difficulties without her daggers.

Naomi gritted her teeth. Three punches, four. It all added up to a horrible pain in her chest that limited her movements. Miko was moving around the guards' heads, tugging and biting at whatever he could. He eventually came back to her though, since he wasn't having much success either.

As a hard kick hit her shin, Naomi stumbled back, but realized too late that there was nothing to stumble back to. All Naomi saw was Heather and Miko also falling, as she hit the harsh waves and fought unconsciousness. Now, her fate was up to the sea, and the only thing left to do was pray that the ruthless sea would be in a surprisingly merciful mood.

Chapter 8: On the Shores of Kry - (Amethyst)

```
Kry: Southern Province, Tashiki
```

Amethyst was not expecting a hug when her eyes opened. She was expecting a lame joke, or a stupid comment, or a quip about her hair. Best said, anything except a hug. Oh, she had never loved her stupid cheapy life, trashy town, disgusting apartment, or mess of a best friend more. Amethyst took a moment to look around and appreciate it. All of it.

They lived on the terrace of an abandoned house that was sandwiched between four other crumbling buildings. Why not just live *inside* the abandoned house? Well, they had tried that, but the ants, cockroaches, and spiders hadn't liked the invasion of their home very much.

Instead, Amethyst and Grek just covered their little apartment with an enormous cloth (featuring several holes) that was tied to a hook on each of the four buildings. This was quite an impressive feat, considering neither of them had ever passed a basic physics class.

Their little house consisted of a lot of old things. Two dirty rugs, each with a ripped blanket and a pillow, acted as beds in one corner of the room. In another corner, there were two buckets (colored bright blue in peeling paint), a tub of water they changed every day, one or two brushes, and a stolen hand soap every once in a while. That was the bathroom, if it wasn't obvious. (And yes, privacy was a nonexistent concept in their "apartment.") Right next to the bathroom stood a wire fence that had come with the old building, useful for hanging the two pairs of clothes that they owned. And lastly, she and Grek had a bunch of boxes where they stored food, plates, and other stuff.

But the best thing it contained was Grek, whose mousy brown hair was currently in her face. Amethyst wheezed in his tight embrace, struggling for breath, but feeling more relaxed in her friend's hug than in a dimension where she couldn't even die. Then Grek let go, but not for long.

"What's wrong with you!?" Grek shouted as he hugged her again. "Don't do that. Don't…" His voice trailed off and Amethyst stared at his hair, untamed and ruffled for one of the first times ever.

What had happened while she was gone?

Wait… for how long was she gone?

"Grek, I'm fine," she reassured him as he grasped her hands.

"I was so worried. You—" Amethyst pulled her hands away from his hold.

"Grek, for how long was I in the vision?" Stress coated every inch of her words, and Amethyst could tell Grek was straining to reply. After a few moments of apprehensive silence, Amethyst repeated herself, louder this time. "Grek, for how long was I gone!?"

"Twenty hours." He responded so quietly that it was practically a whisper.

"Twenty hours!" Amethyst paced around the room, their little shack of a home.

"How long did it feel?"

"I don't know. Five minutes?" Grek ruffled his brown hair, tangling it even further. Whatever had him so shaken had to be important. Before she could ask, Grek continued speaking.

"I don't like to tell you about the amount of time that goes by when you are gone," he began. "Cause if I did, you'd probably notice the same pattern I did."

"Which is?"

"You're sixteen. You have around sixteen visions each year. You always think that they're shorter than they really are, and ever since I've known you, they follow a pattern. They increase by one minute every single time. It would have followed the pattern perfectly, but you were gone too long!" He slipped a timer from his pocket. "Look."

"It could be a coincidence," Amethyst argued.

"It could be intentional."

Then Amethyst remembered what she actually wanted to talk about.

"Grek, my vision was strange," she started.

"Strange how?" he replied. "Aren't your visions always strange?" So, Amethyst told him about King Jiko being in the cave, and how he hid the dragon heir, and Queen Anaji's appearance, and the strange people named Miri and Niki. Grek's puzzled expression was the only real change for the next few seconds.

"Strange, right?" she said.

"Yeah, but who's the dragon heir?"

Amethyst rolled her eyes. "I probably would've told you if I had any clue."

He sighed. "Well, I don't see how this affects us, so just let it be."

"You're right," she replied. "I'm gonna go see if anything washed up on the beach, okay?"

"Alright," Amethyst sighed, hoping, praying, that the long day wasn't about to get any longer.

When she was little, Amethyst had always thought that Kry should clean up their beach and make it a tourist sight. Sadly, not even the locals really enjoyed the beach. Closed-toe shoes were needed because the ground had more glass than sand. Plastic, styrofoam, chairs, toilets, glass bottles, and practically anything else imaginable was on that polluted beach.

Amethyst didn't dare touch the slimy green water, which not even the best painter in the world could capture as "natural." She groaned as a Dumcanpoop (a horrible, *horrible* bird that was native to the Southern Province) pecked at her shoulder. The ghastly birds only had one very unstable leg in the middle of their body, and showed off dull gray and brown feathers, quite like the color of poop. Annoyingly, Dumcanpoops were all blind and relied almost solely on their sense of smell. Amethyst knew very well that their preferred food was garbage, but because of the shocking similarities in smell, Dumcanpoops often confused garbage with humans from Kry.

She couldn't blame them.

The harsh breeze helped distract her from everything that had happened over the past few days: Lodem, her vision, Grek's discovery about her time gaps... It all seemed to be swirling around her mind in an unreadable mess. All this had allowed a thought that had always stayed in the back of her mind, covered up by a million more important things, to reemerge: her past.

Because no matter how many times she had told Grek that she didn't care why her hair was black and white, that her past didn't matter to her, that she didn't mind not knowing where her parents were, or if they were alive, she was lying. It did. She was sick of the unfinished puzzle that her life was. She was sick of not remembering anything that had happened in the first three years of her existence.

Of course, she would get little flashbacks every now and then. There was one image of a man in a cape, and another picture where a witch queen in a lab watched as black serums ran out of little tubes. Her first cohesive memories started around the time she was four.

A horrid old woman with lavender hair and a giant wart on her nose had been her guardian when she was little. How she happened to end up there, Amethyst didn't know, but this woman's face was the first that she could recognize. She wore random dish rags as clothing, and rarely moved from her mattress, often yelling at Amethyst: "Get me some more tequila, you worthless little girl! Or you won't get anything at all!"

But what Amethyst most remembered about this woman was the odd, swirl-shaped tattoo on her neck.

She now looked upon the little shed where she and this woman used to live out on the beach. It had been overtaken by the sea, but this woman's death wasn't so natural.

Three men came into the house a few days after her eighth birthday, dressed in black and crimson, and they too had the tattoo that Amethyst had found so strange on the old woman's neck. The old woman had pleaded and bargained, but the men kept saying the same thing, over and over again: "You have a debt to repay."

That was when the young Amethyst had walked through the door, and the old woman smiled. She said: "Fine, you can take her instead of me. She will be more useful to you anyway." The men nodded, and they gave her some time to pack up her things. During that time, the old woman had asked for one final drink.

"Little girl, will you at least be useful for once and serve me my last tequila coming from you?"

"Okay," Amethyst had said. Then she looked at the three men. "Would any of you like tequila?"

"Yes," they replied.

And Amethyst had given them a tequila, alright, with a few drops of a tiny bottle with a skull and an x on it that the old woman had stored in a cupboard. Then, she left the drinks on the table and rushed to the bathroom, saying that it was an emergency. From there, she jumped out the window and ran. Her head spun in circles. What was next? She had gotten herself out of one problem; what about the next? What if she was alone for the rest of her life, with no one who actually cared? Would there be more men with tattoos and old women in rags trying to hurt her?

Would more people make her feel worthless? Was she?

Eight-year-old Amethyst was disappointed, though, because she eventually had to learn that there were a lot of nasty people in the world. And for people like her, feeling worthless was pretty common. However, neither the three men nor the old woman ever bothered her again.

Amethyst shook herself from the memory and picked up a poster that was caught between a few rocks and read aloud the nearly illegible words on the deteriorated parchment.

"Thirty people Lost in the newest time gap." Amethyst despised the word *Lost*, or at least its relation with time gaps. *Lost* was just a sugar-coated term for *killed in a time gap*. Those people were as dead as Grek's little sister, and no amount of searching would ever bring them back.

As Amethyst lowered the poster, her eyes caught sight of three more horrors.

One: a limping Valaztenian snow monkey who appeared to have his eyes open.

Two: an unconscious girl with flaming crimson hair that looked exactly like Grek's description of his little sister.

Three: a woman with raven black hair and light brown skin, immediately recognizable to anyone with half a brain as the dead princess of Valaztein.

Amethyst sprinted as fast as she could towards Grek, afraid that the three figures' fragile breathing would end soon. Yelling at people to get out of her way, Amethyst finally reached the pub where (thankfully) a sober Grek awaited her. She yanked at his arm and gave him a very quick overview of what she had seen on the beach. He ran even faster at the mention of his little sister, and Amethyst found herself struggling to keep up with him.

Once they reached the beach, they had to work fast if they wanted to save anyone.

"Grek," she said. "Get the princess and I'll grab the girl and the monkey." Amethyst could only imagine that he was nodding, because she didn't take the time to inspect his expression. She hauled the red-headed girl over her shoulder and grabbed the snow monkey with her free arm. She then ran back to the village, all the weight slowing her.

Finally, they reached their room. The monkey seemed to be getting better, but the princess and the redhead were barely breathing. She and Grek didn't waste a second.

"CPR," Grek said, and Amethyst obeyed. She wasn't sure where Grek had learned CPR, but he had taught her and Amethyst had deemed it an incredibly useful skill. Amethyst started on the princess and Grek did the redhead. She did the first few presses and breathed.

Nothing.

Three more times.

Nothing.

Again.

Nothing.

"Damn it!" Amethyst cursed as she repeated the process.

Nothing.

One more time.

A stream of water came pouring out of the princess's mouth, and several coughs followed that. Amethyst glanced at Grek and saw he was having the same success. Looking back at the girl, she saw that a large cascade of blood was rushing down the princess's thigh to her calf.

"Amethyst, do you…"

"Get the bandages!" Grek grabbed several from their meager supply and they both began placing it on the princess's leg. Amethyst sighed as the heavy rush of blood was reduced to a small trickle. The redhead's eyes opened and she seemed to finally be getting her bearings. She then looked up at Grek and her entire expression shifted to one of wonder and disbelief.

"Grek?" she stuttered.

"Heather?" They both nodded, and Amethyst witnessed her best friend and a stranger wrap into a teary embrace.

Chapter 9: Where the Seas Led - (Naomi)

```
Kry: Southern Province, Tashiki
```

When Naomi awoke, everything was blurry. Since both her senses of smell and hearing were also disoriented, she tried to move her arm to check if she was bleeding or, well, dead. Even through her blurry vision, she didn't appear to be in heaven at all. All she could make out was a figure hovering over her and a weird tent thing that had ripped and brown spots. At least, she thought they were brown. They could've been pink for all the good her sight was doing.

When her arm finally moved, and Naomi's hand touched a bunch of bandages on her leg, she realized that she was alive. Alive, and apparently, somehow not bleeding. After a few more minutes, her sight came into focus and so did her hearing, but maybe not her smell, because the air was full with a thick odor of garbage.

"It smells like…" Naomi's voice trailed off.

"Garbage?" replied one of the figures hovering over her. So, it was real. Her eyes immediately went to the figure who spoke. The girl was in her teens, probably only a few years younger than Naomi. She had light skin, blue eyes, and a small nose, but by far her most striking feature was the equal strips of black and white hair that covered her head. Then, everything went spiraling back to her, and Naomi burst into a long rush of questions.

"Did Miranda send you? Do you want to kill me? Where's Heather? And Miko? Are they okay? Am I in the capital? Where's Ez?" The girl shushed her before she could continue.

"Let's start with: aren't you supposed to be dead?"

Naomi blinked. "What?"

"Sorry," said the girl. "I'm Amethyst. You're in Kry. The Queen of Valaztein told everyone you're dead." Dead? How would that be beneficial to... Of course! If Naomi was dead, the rebellion was squashed.

"Where are Heather and Miko?"

"With Grek."

"Who's Grek?"

"Me, darling," said a man as he walked up to her. His hazel hair glimmered in the afternoon sun, and his caramel-colored eyes reached out to her with a severely annoying charm.

Naomi suddenly felt very perturbed that he hadn't chosen to wear a shirt. As he tried to kiss her hand, Amethyst interrupted.

"Back off, Grek. She's way out of your league." Amethyst twirled her hair. "Just like me."

Grek imitated a fake laugh and rolled his eyes. What would it be like to have a friend like that? Someone her age she could talk to? Naomi wondered. The closest person she had gotten to that was Prince Crescent's younger sister, Crystal. Even then, Naomi wasn't allowed to play with her much because it wasn't as "beneficial" as playing with Crescent was.

Naomi made out a figure a few meters away from her and realized that it was Heather. Her face lit up in joy.

"Come on, sis," the one named Grek said as he motioned to Heather. "She's awake." *Sis?* Naomi thought. *Heather never mentioned that she had a brother.*

The fourteen-year-old ran towards her with Miko on her shoulder, but Naomi was too preoccupied puzzling over Grek's words to pay much attention. The moment Heather reached Naomi, she appeared to see that too, because her face twisted into a weak fake smile. Naomi sounded way too much like a scolding teacher when she said it, but her curiosity was too strong to resist.

"Heather, I think you have some explaining to do."

Amethyst and Grek were patiently waiting outside of the room sipping at drinks, while Naomi and Heather were each seated on a small cushion. Miko had decided to take a little nap on Naomi's lap, and every few minutes he'd hoot or squeal, deep in a dream. For a while, there was silence. Heather didn't want to speak; Naomi didn't know how to. So, she just sat there, quiet and curious as all the vendors yelled and haggled on the street, selling anything from gold and silver to exotic animals. The climate was dry, sandy hot, and unforgiving, and Naomi was not used to it. A few moments later, Heather finally said something.

"Okay, maybe I have a brother. So what? I don't have to tell you everything."

"You're right," Naomi replied. "You don't. But since I don't know the first thing about you, other than that you tried to kill me, I'd appreciate a little hint."

"Fine. My childhood sucked, alright? Usual sob story: loving family, dead parent. And then I was taken from my family, including Grek, and I didn't think it would be relevant to tell you any of this because it was extremely unlikely for me to ever see him again, got it?"

Naomi nodded. "Sorry for asking."

"Don't be." Heather popped a piece of gum in her mouth. "You don't know the half of it."

Naomi caressed Miko's fur, not sure what to do with the information that she had been handed. It was so unclear that it could mean practically anything. She was "taken from her family"? By whom? Why? Regardless, it wasn't like Heather was the comforting type.

Naomi sighed. She had to focus on more important things, like finding the people of the Elemento Tribe Territories and getting to the prince. Because Heather was a code that she wasn't going to crack anytime soon.

Chapter 10: The Original Sin - (Ez)

```
Sindí: Southern Province, Tashiki
```

Ez was pulled (against his will) from the edge of the boat, but his eyes never left the water, searching, praying for a face he knew would never come.

Naomi, Naomi, Naomi.

What if she was dead? Or worse: Miranda had found her? What was her plan in coming all the way out here anyway? Was she alone? Well, at least that question had an easy answer: no. This was Naomi; she always tried to save people, no matter the cost.

"Come on," Ariah said as she continued dragging him. "We're arriving in Sindí in a few hours. You're gonna cause suspicion."

They started to walk towards their room, other soldiers watching them eerily. *Oh, great. As if I need another bunch of people on my tail.* But despite the spying looks and the million tasks he was supposed to be doing on the boat, Ez kept coming back to one thing.

"She shouldn't have brought them with her."

Ariah gave him only a puzzled expression. "What?"

"She must have brought Valazteinian civilians with her. By the looks of it, thousands," Ez explained.

"So she got on the ship to disable the radiation system?"

"Why else?" He jogged down the wooden stairs that led to their quarters, biting his lip.

Heck, Naomi's empathy was gonna get her killed. Maybe he could send someone to find her, just to make sure she was safe. There was an agent he knew, someone who owed him a favor. "This is a disaster."

Ariah laughed. "I know quite a bit about disasters."

"I bet you do," he muttered under his breath. Ariah obviously heard him, but strolled ahead of him instead of responding. She opened the door that led to their room and fell onto her bed. A few seconds later, she looked up.

"I've given up waiting for you to forgive me, so we can stop having these conversations." Then she lay back down again.

Ez scoffed. "You know, you haven't apologized once. Never."

"What difference would it make? It's not like it would change your opinion."

He curled his fists. She was unbelievable! "Only you would say something like that. I bet you wouldn't even change what you did if you could go back there."

"Killing my mother, probably not the best decision. But my deal with Miranda? No way I would change it. If it were the same circumstances, the same consequences… I'd do it again in a heartbeat."

Should he cry, laugh, or scream?! "What consequences? What could Miranda have ever offered you that would be worth what you did?"

"You'd never understand."

He moved his head. Just the sight of her was painful. "Why are you here?" he finally said. "I know you helped me escape and all, but why?" The answer was probably nothing he wanted to hear. Most likely, she was on a mission from the Queen or had to track him down, and maybe kill some government official from Tashiki on the way. Something like that.

Unfortunately, the ship's docking alert responded before Ariah could.

"Come on," she said. "We better keep moving. What does your little necklace say?"

Ez slipped the amulet out of his satchel. While they'd been on the boat, the gemstone had changed colors considerably, going from red to orange to a pukish yellow as they neared the shore. He moved it around, pointing the gem in all directions until it finally turned green.

"East," Ez said. "That's what it says."

"What's east?"

"The Myi Woods, apparently. I stole a pocket map from the boat."

The shuffling of feet was the prominent sound as the ship arrived in Tashiki and everyone hurried to leave. No wonder. The ocean was a preferred wonder to him, but claustrophobic ship compartments that weren't big enough to house a mouse's family, much less two people, weren't. The port was outrageously odorous, quite small to be one of the only ports in the Southern Province of Tashiki, and only connected to the ship by a large plank of wobbly wood, which he was quite sure at least three people had already fallen off of. Ariah nudged at his arm.

"Keep your head low, move fast, and don't bring attention to yourself, got it?"

"Got it."

"Follow me." Ariah led him across the wooden plank easily, and the rest was pretty simple.

Actually, Ez was surprised by how small the city of Sindí really was. In forty-five minutes, they had already passed through most of the city on foot, and more rural terrain began to reveal itself. When she realized it was safe to talk, Ariah asked, "Ez, what are we doing in the Southern Province? There's a risk of time gaps here."

"I'm well aware." Ez pulled his pocket map out. "But the stupid amulet thought otherwise."

"Fine." Ariah snatched the map and inspected their distance from the woods. "Should be a few hours."

"Okay." He inspected a nearby selling booth. "Shouldn't we get a flashlight or something?"

"Probably." They walked over to the booth, where a young woman with slick black hair, maybe thirty-five at most, stood staring at the setting sun.

"Do you have a pair of flashlights?" Ez asked. "We're setting off for the Myi Woods."

The woman's expression twisted and her eyes were like flashlights themselves, flickering and panicking.

"The Myi Woods?" Her voice was quivering. Why was she so terrified? All he knew about the Myi Woods was that "woods" was a misidentification, because the wildlife was mostly monkeys, Dumcanpoops, and frogs.

"What's wrong with the Myi Woods?" Ariah questioned, her gaze oddly unrelenting. Ez then remembered that among her many jobs at the dragon base, Ariah used to interrogate high-ranking prisoners. This, of course, meant breaking them until they cracked. Because that was just Ariah's way of doing things: hit until it breaks. If the woman was scared before, she sure as hell was scared now.

"Don't you know the legend?" she whispered. They both shook their heads. "Well, they say that the woods are haunted by the ghost of a young boy whose sister was taken by bandits, and his one fear—"

"That's enough legends for now, thank you," Ez interrupted, annoyed that such valuable time was being wasted at the hand of ghost stories that should be told at a twelve-year-old girl's sleepover.

***

The Myi Woods were not quiet, nor would they probably ever be. Every time silence tried to break through, it was interrupted by the rush of a river, or the hoots from twenty annoying monkeys, or the eerie rustling of the wind in the leaves, or a frog croak, or anything else in the world. However, the most annoying thing about the Myi Woods was undoubtedly the pinkas, bird-like creatures with colorful baby blue and hot pink feathers that heard a word and mimicked it endlessly. For someone who just desired some peace and quiet to process everything, it was infuriating.

To top this, the Myi Woods seemed to be the only place in all of the Southern Province that wasn't as dry as a desert. In fact, the slushing of his boots against the mucky ground made almost as much sound as the chaotic wildlife. Moss covered every inch of the peeling, leafless Linoe trees and the dying plants. How could a place so rich with wildlife and filled with water be dying?

"Why's everything so dead?" Ez asked.

"'Cause this rainforest became a disposal for sewage water ever since the king stopped helping the people of the Southern Province," Ariah replied, disgusted.

Ez tried to ignore everything he hated about the Myi Woods, and instead, his thoughts wandered to the one person who recently filled his mind every waking moment he allowed it to wander. For that same reason, he liked to keep vigorous control over his thoughts. Fury flamed inside of him, right next to the even larger problem that was worry. Why did Naomi have to keep trying to save everyone? She could so easily flee on her own; she'd never get caught. Instead, she'd once again started martyring herself to help people. This would be a repetition of the Crown Maze accident; he knew it. He just had to pray, pray to whatever monster was supervising his life… that she'd come out alive.

"This looks like a good camping site, right?" Ariah asked.

Ez barely turned his head. "What?"

She smacked him hard on the cheek and reality came back into focus. "Right?"

He was standing under the cover of a few Linoe trees, where his feet sank into some mushy soil, and a small river could be seen a few yards away.

"Yeah, it looks perfect. I'll take the first watch."

"No point. There's nothing here," Ariah said. Slowly, but eventually, Ez drifted into a restless sleep.

"Damn it!" Ez was awoken from his sleep by Ariah's angry yelling.

"What..."

She threw something at the mushy floor. "Someone took our food! We've got sixty miles to go out of this forest and we have no food or water!"

"Calm down, Ar—"

"I'm going to kill whoever did this!"

Suddenly, Ez was reminded of the days at the dragon base, before Ariah's betrayal.

Before everything. They were thirteen and on a mission through the freezing mountains of Lightmoon. There had been no time like it.

The snow was falling on the icy mountain, and even Ez's three fur and leather jackets couldn't keep him warm. All he could see when he looked down from their steep path was a blizzard below the clouds, and hail shooting down at the world below like knives of crystal.

"Why the heck is it so cold up here?" thirteen-year-old him had asked.

"Gee, I dunno..." Ariah replied. "Maybe 'cause we're 25,000 feet up?!" Suddenly, she crumbled to the floor. Her face lost all color and her brown eyes took on a grayish tint.

"Ariah?!" Ez said, his voice quivering.

"I'm fine." She tried to get up, but could barely move her arms.

"No, you're not." He picked her up and carried her along the path, hoping and praying for any kind of little cave or opening in the mountain. Between Ariah's weight on his arms and the supplies he was carrying on his back, Ez was well aware that he wouldn't be able to continue at this pace for long. Finally, they found a cave in the mountain, and he laid her down. With some wood and flint he had in his satchel, Ez made a fire next to her, and melted some snow into water.

"Ez, really, you don't have to—"

"Just drink."

So she did, and they stayed there for a few hours until Ariah could breathe again, nestled in the warmth of their coats.

"Ez?" she asked as they began walking out of the cave to continue. "Can you carry my things for me? I'm sorry, I thought I could, but I can't."

"Yeah, sure," he replied. Ez strapped her bags across his shoulder and they continued up the mountain, hand in hand.

"I can't believe your mom sent us here alone," Ez said as he stepped across an icy ledge. "She barely trusts us with a regional mission. I bet she just couldn't get the adults to do it."

"You give yourself too little credit. You know, we're already at the highest level for our age. Someday we're going to be her best agents. Period."

"Well, at lea—" Ez slipped on the ice, his body dangling three hundred feet above a frosted canyon. "Help!" Ariah snatched his wrist, straining to hold up his weight. The satchels slipped off Ez's back, leaving all their supplies stranded in the icy wasteland below.

"Oh, my..." Ariah muttered under her breath. "Just hold on!"

"Okay!"

After a few minutes of struggling, she managed to pull him up, and they both stared at the empty distance, wondering where their supplies could be, and how in the world they were going to survive without them.

That was when Ariah started to break. "Oh gosh. We're gonna die. Ez! We're gonna die!"

"Calm down. It's going to be okay. Just brea—"

"We're gonna die on a freezing mountain, and no one's gonna bury us, because we were the only people crazy enough to get up here!"

Ez grabbed her shoulder and turned her towards him. "Ariah, we're going to get through this. We have plenty of fresh snow, which means that we have plenty of drinkable water. Plus, we can survive over a week without food, and we'll get to a supply stop in only a few days."

"But that won't matter if we freeze to death!" she yelled.

He pulled her into a hug. "We're not gonna freeze. We have enough layers to keep us alive, okay?"

"Yes, yes, I guess you're right. I'm sorry I freaked out."

"Don't be. It's a perfectly normal reaction."

"Let's get to it then," Ariah said.

They pulled away from their tight embrace and continued trudging up the mountain. They didn't stop walking for days, focused only on their destination. When one of them wanted to give up, the other wouldn't let it happen. They talked and laughed and, most of all, never let go of each other's hands.

As they were starving and freezing and barely alive, Ez said, "Well, we're never gonna want to come back to this moment again."

And back in the present, Ez could only think of how wrong thirteen-year-old him had been. He could only think of how much he wished that he could go back there again, and relive every moment of that crazy, dangerous, life-threatening experience, because it reminded him of who he had been: a fighter. A friend. A hero.

This time, as Ariah continued freaking out about the loss of their food, a voice startled them.

"Sorry," a voice interjected from a distance.

"Where did that come from?" Ariah asked, reaching for the knife that she kept in her pocket. Then, a little boy, no older than eleven, appeared from a clump of trees behind them. His warm brown skin was shiny with sweat from the heat, and his messy dreadlocks swished frequently, because he seemed to be moving every half a second. Though precautionary, Ez grabbed Ariah and made sure she didn't reach for her knife.

"The monkeys can get naughty sometimes," the boy said. "Of course, you don't want to be anywhere near Hulu or Nono when they're hungry. On second thought, you should watch out for Meimei too. Don't be too harsh on them though, 'kay? Cause I think Nono may have a traumatic condition or something. Honestly, I don't blame him. There's been this whole thing with the frogs. I mean, I try to keep the peace, but it's like a civil war around here. BOOM! First cannon fired. At least the pinkas are calm. They help keep the peace around here, even if they have a little contest with the monkeys to see who is louder. Anyways, I hope you don't mind the mushiness. It's really mushy this time of year, well, it's mushy every time of year, but especia—"

Ariah shoved a clump of moss into his mouth.

"Does he ever stop talking?"

The boy spit out the clump of moss. "I like to think I have very resistant vocal cords."

"No kidding," Ariah muttered.

"So, what's your name, kid?" Ez asked.

"Oh, right. My name's Daunt. I'm ten years old. I like blue and I like green, but only forest green, that pale disaster looks like puke. Yellow's real pretty too. My favorite animal is impossible to choose, 'cause I love all—"

"I asked for your name. Not your life story," Ez replied. "I'm Ez. This is Ariah."

"Cool! Nice to meet ya!" Daunt held out his hand in a high-five position. Of course, Ariah didn't even lift a finger. "Come on! Don't leave me hanging." Her hand didn't move, and Daunt finally lowered his arm, frowning.

"Don't take it personally, kid. She leaves everyone hanging, often quite literally." Ariah glared at him, he glared back, and Daunt's gaze was as far away from them and as close to the floor as possible. Well, at least the kid could read the room.

"That was fun. Anyway…" Daunt continued. "I know where the best mango and pineapple trees are. Trust me, they are delicious!"

"That's great, but we won't be taking any more help from you," Ariah stated as she walked away, trying to move quickly, but failing because of the sinking ground.

Daunt glanced at Ez and whispered, "Does she always have anger issues?"

"No," he whispered back. "Just every few seconds."

"Come on, Ariah," Ez said, grabbing her arm. "We need food. Plus, the kid's really sweet."

"Sweet?" she scoffed. "Try annoying."

"Ariah…"

"Fine." She pointed at Daunt. "Lead the way, Ghost Boy."

"Oh, Ghost Boy. That's a cute little rumor. You know who started it: Emily. Funny little monkey. Joined a frog reporter and leaked information to the press. That's how the legend started. You know, I kind of miss humans. Might stick around a bit longer with you guys. You know…"

Ez let all Daunt's jumbled chit-chat fade to merely a background noise, like the rush of a nearby river, or the squawking of a pinka, all the while processing one overarching thought about Daunt's chatter: *spare me*.

When they arrived at their next camping ground, Daunt tried to teach them how to crochet a pillow out of moss, which ended in Ariah and Ez using the lumpy pillows that Daunt, and only Daunt, had made. Two large Tink trees covered their spot, and they could see glimpses of sun behind the fuzzy pea-green leaves. Ez and Ariah sat down next to their pillows, eating some bread that Daunt had given them.

"I'll be right back," Ez said. "I have to use the restroom."

Ez walked away from their campsite and to a nearby tree. With him, he brought Miranda's diary, and he started reading it.

So what? He had told a white lie. A few feet of distance would keep Daunt snooping around his bag and Ariah from sneaking any information to Miranda. It was better this way. The first entry read:

Dear Diary,

Um…hi? Okay, this feels kinda stupid, but apparently it can help with my "issues." I guess I should introduce myself. Hello, I'm

Miranda, and I am twelve years old to date. So... my dad's a psycho who locks me up in my room at night, but I guess he means well, right? Uh, I don't know. What I do know is that his new wife is crazy. Empress Zylena of Xoman, or whatever. She has tried to convince him to get rid of me on several occasions because of "them." I should probably explain that here. I have a weird little... ability. I can control my shadow, and I bet I could control other people's shadows too, if I tried. But I don't really control my powers: he does. His name is Azure, the god of shadows, and he works with the Shadow Council. They're kind of like a bad nightmare, but every night they change me; they make me someone I'm not.

That's all for today, I think. Sincerely,

Miranda.

It felt so strange to see Miranda in that light: young, vulnerable. The little girl in this letter was unrecognizable... nothing like the monster who had created an army of children. There was still a lot to process, but Ariah and Daunt would come looking for him if he didn't start heading back soon. So, he arrived back at the campground and found Ariah with an obvious expression of pain and boredom on her face.

"So, how's life?" the little boy asked.

"Same as the last twenty times you asked," Ariah replied, turning her head as she saw Ez. "Hey, hope your little getaway was nice but we've got a problem." Uh, the last thing they needed was another complication.

"What?"

"The gemstone went backward," Ariah said.

"How?" Ez rushed towards Ariah, too mad and confused to yell at Ariah for going through his stuff.

"How should I know? Maybe your mythical beast took a road trip," she replied. "It was almost blue and now it's green again."

"They couldn't have gone far. We should hit Kry tomorrow. We'll ask around there."

"So, how do you two know each other?" Daunt interrupted, trying to stir up some unneeded and unwanted small talk.

"She killed my family," Ez said bluntly.

Ariah punched him in the arm. "Great conversation starter."

"Just telling the truth, but I guess that concept is unknown to you, rat."

Ariah plastered on a fake smile as she whispered in his ear, "Well, I'm sure that murdering your parents is much better."

"It *is* better!" Ez said. "I only killed two people, and it was for a cause. You killed hundreds because you were a selfish, entitled, insecure teenager who wanted to mean something! Well congratulations, I bet you mean a lot to the families of all the people whose lives you ended."

"You are just taking random guesses on a topic you don't know anything about!"

"Does anyone have popcorn?" Daunt asked.

They both glared at him.

"Can you go away?" Ariah demanded. "You're like fleas."

"Why would I go away?" he responded. "I haven't had entertainment in quite a long time, and I've got front-row seats to this."

Then Ez proceeded to do what all annoyed people would: ignore him.

"Then explain it," he told Ariah. She held her breath for at least ten seconds before continuing.

"Fine. I'll explain it to you. Ez, where was I when we were staging Naomi's capture?"

"In the Queen's dungeons as a dragon decoy," he replied.

"Dragons?" Daunt interrupted. "This should be a comic book."

"And where were you?" Ariah asked.

"In the Queen's dungeons as well."

"Since that was my nearest visit to the Queen before the massacre, is it safe to assume that that's when I made the deal?"

"Yes," he replied, suddenly fitting the pieces together.

"And what do you think the Queen would do to you if I didn't?"

"Ariah…"

"Secondly, Eppeye. Do you agree that the massacre took place during your time in Eppeye?" Ariah asked.

"Yes." The pieces were beginning to fit together, and Ez did not like the reality of this puzzle.

"And who do you think, Ez, sent you on the mission to Eppeye?"

"You," he replied.

"Correct."

"Ariah," he started. "You know this doesn't begin to pardon you for what you've done."

"I know," she replied. "At the very most, it answers your question."

Chapter 11: Sweat and Tears - (Amethyst)

Southern Province: Tashiki

Tired and hungry, Amethyst sat around the makeshift table that she and Grek had made out of a cardboard box in her tiny room. On the table, Amethyst eagerly awaited the two pieces of stale bread, the can of beans, and the bottle of whiskey that they had stolen that day. Two other people eyed the food with her, awaiting Grek, who was taking forever to fix his hair. Oh! And a snow monkey. How did the monkey fit into everything again?

A few seconds later, Grek came back and said, "What did I miss?"

"We have to find the prince," Naomi urged, as Amethyst dug into the food. "My people are headed towards the capital illegally, and with no official leadership that the prince will listen to. Besides, we have to change his mind while he's still in the interim."

"There's a slight problem with that," Grek told Naomi.

"Other than the fact that he's a self-entitled rich manchild who probably won't listen to anyone but himself?" Amethyst cut in.

Grek rolled his eyes at her, and Amethyst grinned. It was nice to see that some things didn't change.

"So what's the reason?" Heather asked.

"Grek, why don't you tell them?" Amethyst replied. "You're better at this stuff than I am anyways."

"Okay," he said. "You know the whole four provinces thing, right?"

"Yes," Naomi replied. "The Western Province is the main agricultural zone, the Eastern Province is the main port, and the Northern Province is very, very wealthy."

"Yeah, pretty much," Amethyst replied as she tried to open a can of beans.

"A couple of years ago," Grek explained. "Maybe a little more than twenty, time gaps started appearing, but only in the Southern Province."

"I've gotten that far," said Naomi.

"What you probably don't know," Amethyst cut in. "is that fifteen years ago, when the time gap disaster was still a pretty new mess-up, the *wonderful* King Jiko"—the words were coated with a thick layer of sarcasm—"decided to release an official mandate stating that anyone who wished to leave the Southern Province had to pay a mandatory fee."

"How much?" Heather asked from the other corner of the room.

"Two-thousand dellum," Amethyst replied.

"Dellum!?" Naomi shouted. "So, what are we gonna do?"

"We?" Grek said. "Wait a minute, dead princess, what makes you think that we want to go with you?"

"Perhaps the fact that you would be helping to end a deadly war in Valaztein that could potentially affect the entire world if we don't get to the prince now?"

"You see," Grek continued. "Our life already sucks, so if you promise us more suckiness, we won't really care. If you promise us that things could possibly get *better*... You know... money, status"—he looked around, inspecting the town of Kry—"relocation, maybe we'd be more willing."

Naomi scoffed. "Gosh, you really are thugs. I'll be the Queen of Valaztein. I'll have a lot of money, blah, blah blah. Thirty thousand dellum."

Grek's jaw dropped. Amethyst could see the thoughts spiraling through his head. Thirty thousand dellum? With thirty thousand dellum he could do anything! Move out of Kry, buy a nice house... Still, Grek's personality wouldn't let him leave it at that.

"Forty thousand dellum and we'll call it a deal." At that point, Amethyst yanked his wrist and dragged her friend outside. "Ow!" Grek said once they were on the street. "What was that for?"

"Are you insane? We don't even know this girl!"

"Amethyst, have you looked at her? The dead-princess-of-Valaztein face is kinda hard to miss!"

"I guess so," Amethyst replied with a sigh.

"What's really going on?" Grek wrapped his arm around her, his style of a friendly hug.

"Do you really think anything's going to change?"

"Of course it is! Just getting out of this place will be a game changer."

"How can you believe that? After a lifetime of being treated like dirt... what could it matter where we go? All they see is this."

Amethyst pointed at her hair. "And this." she signaled at the dirt smudges on her face. "And this too." The tattoo seared across her entire arm from when she'd been indebted to the wrong people. "I stopped searching for respect a long time ago. Maybe you should too."

"What do you care about their respect? Don't let anyone else let you think you're dirt. We don't belong here."

"We don't belong anywhere." Amethyst wiped a tear from her face and then Grek pinched her cheek. "Ouch!"

"Snap out of it!" he said. "We're gonna make it, you and me. We're gonna get that snowy gold mansion." Grek gave her a big hug. "We belong somewhere, together. Until you find your white prince, of course."

Amethyst chuckled. "Never."

"Are you ready to try again?"

"I am." With that, they walked up to the "apartment."

When they came back, Naomi was discussing something with Heather in a hushed voice. Made sense that a princess didn't think her conversation was trivial enough for common peasants. Uh, rich people.

"Forty thousand is ridiculous," Naomi said.

Grek's little sister turned to Naomi. "I can't leave him. He's my brother."

"Fine. Forty thousand dellum."

"Deal," Grek said. A handshake later, the entire room was in agreement as to where they were going and why.

That was when Amethyst realized something. There was more than one reason for her to go to the palace. If she could just locate where the site of her vision was, which was probably somewhere in the palace, she could find out who Niki and Miri were.

"But how are we going to get across the border?" Grek asked. "It's not like one of us has two thousand dellum just lying around."

Naomi looked both grim and determined as she spoke her next few words. "Something called Dark magic."

At five the next morning, the sky was deep blue and burnt orange. The amber-colored sun tried to push its way through the smokey clouds that filled the morning sunrise. Despite the sleepy atmosphere though, Kry was very much awake. Vendors yelled at travelers in carriages. And the hazardous road traffic still provided the aggravated horse neighs and human shouts that characterized the place Amethyst had learned to call home.

After ten minutes of walking, they found a carriage pulled over by the side of the road. This was no stroke of luck, though; cab drivers in Kry were some of the most irresponsible people in the world. They'd leave their carriages unguarded to stop for snacks, or hit them against a street pole and run so that the government "cops" wouldn't see them.

As Heather untied the horses, Grek went straight to the trunk to check for alcohol. *Of course he would.* It was very, incredibly Grek to do that.

"Sweet!" he yelled. "Does anyone like whiskey?" Amethyst rushed to get the bottle out of his hand.

"Give me that!" Amethyst said as she snatched it. She walked toward a neon-yellow trash can, sure that she was going to make some partying teenager very excited.

"Don't!" Heather said. "Right now, we don't have enough money to buy a first aid kit, so we can use whiskey as a disinfectant."

Amethyst blinked. "Huh?"

"To clean wounds," Heather explained.

"Oh, okay." She strolled away from the trash can, keeping the bottle of whiskey as close to her as possible. "Fine, but I'll keep it in my bag, and Grek doesn't even get close to it."

They were all busy preparing the carriage, so no one really answered her, but the promise Amethyst had made was more for herself than anyone else. She was going to help her best friend, no matter how little help he wanted.

A few minutes later, the carriage was ready to go, and Amethyst settled in the front with Naomi. Naomi didn't know the streets of Kry, Grek should never be trusted with a driver's position, and Heather was too young to even get a license. (Which, if she was being honest, didn't really matter in Kry.) Anyway, Amethyst drove the carriage by a process of elimination, and Naomi sat beside her, watching everything in silence. It took them over three hours, but they finally made it to the border, where a giant steel fence towered above a little wooden kiosk. There, a man with dark skin and gray eyes looked extremely bored.

Naomi jumped off from the carriage. Wait, what was she doing? Was the woman insane? The man would recognize her as the rebel princess of Valaztein in two seconds and their mission would be done!

"My name is Minami Chaine. Me and my friends would like to cross the border."

"Wait, but you're..." The man checked his clipboard, but by then Naomi had already started her transformation. First, her lively green eyes turned a deathly black. Her veins bulged out of her skin, indigo and monstrous. It was like all life was getting sucked out of Naomi... voluntarily.

The next part was worse. The shadows pulled upwards, reaching, reaching for the man's mind.

"Ahh!" he screamed

"Shh," Naomi hushed. "I'm not going to hurt you. You're just going to feel a little bit tired after this."

"I don't want to die today," the man whimpered towards the sky.

"You won't," Naomi said. And then, for a moment, the black-eyed princess glanced back at Amethyst and the rest of them, whispering one silent phrase before everything went quiet.

"Close your eyes."

Amethyst did, and waited until far after the bang of the gate unbolting resonated in her ears before she opened her eyes again. The man looked fine. He was back at the kiosk waiting for the next request, which Amethyst doubted would ever come. No one in the Southern Province had that kind of money.

No one.

She then inspected Naomi, who looked, well... unreadable. She always did. What had happened in her past? What had made her so stiff, so armed? Through what she could see, Naomi was like a well-guarded fortress, unyielding to any kind of cannon or weapon. The only real way Amethyst saw that she could be hurt was well... from the inside.

And beyond that Amethyst needed to know... how could someone born believing she's the world's finest be so kind? Despite all the status she held (being a literal princess), Naomi had never held her head high or made Amethyst feel like trash. And she was going to figure out why.

So, Amethyst determined she would be the very first person to knock at the gates of that grand fortress.

The traveling was hard, but not much harder than what Amethyst had been accustomed to. They slept mostly in makeshift tents or out in the open grass, because they had agreed that going through the wilderness would be the fastest and safest option. Of course, the wild had its downsides. For example, Grek's lungs had reacted poorly to the clean air. He was coughing and choking all over the place. It was like his lungs missed dust. Weird. Somehow, it got him even more hooked on those god-forsaken Tashiki cigarettes.

Thankfully, they'd found a nice sleeping arrangement tonight. An abandoned wooden cabin gave them a little extra warmth as the animals howled on in the harsh winter night.

However, one thing was made clear throughout all her time sleeping near Naomi: the girl didn't sleep. Even during the rare five-minute patches where Naomi did, it was restless, tossing and turning, and tossing and turning. And she'd always, always, wake up sweating and barely breathing, scouting around and making sure Heather and Miko were still there.

Naomi was always first on watch and took at least two watches per night. It was practically inhuman, the way she never let her guard down. Amethyst would take one or two watches every few nights, and even then, she would cheat a little. Her powers were very useful for tedious tasks like being on guard. All it took was a few minutes of concentration and she could fast-forward time five, eight, sometimes even ten minutes if she really tried.

Amethyst walked up to the princess during one of her watches and the two sat silently, watching the black sky, the few stars out making no impact at all. The rest of their group was sleeping in an abandoned wooden cabin that they had found, but it was better to do the watch from outside.

"Couldn't sleep either?" Naomi finally asked.

"Yeah." Lies. She was only curious.

"Why can't you sleep?" Naomi asked.

Oh, no more questions. "I dunno. Just confused about all this stuff. Grek, Heather, you. You know, alive." That was all true, though.

Naomi chuckled. "Yes, it's not exactly easy, is it?"

Amethyst paused. "Not even a little bit. But it helps to remember the good things, especially the new ones. What's the best thing that's happened to you lately?"

"Heather," Naomi responded, quick as a bullet. "You?"

"Well," she began. "I met this guy at the tax co—"

Naomi smiled for a moment, as if remembering something beautiful, and a small touch of humanity filled her gaze. Then, she got up from her sitting position, looked out at the horizon and said, "Don't waste your time. Love's not worth it."

Amethyst didn't even have time to process her words, because just as Naomi said them, Amethyst felt an itching heat at her back. She turned around and stared. Stared at the wild flames that were engulfing the cabin.

Chapter 12: The Approaching - (Urumi)

(Capital)Mae Lì: Northern Province, Tashiki

Urumi sat on a white porcelain chair on the marbled balcony of the palace, looking out at the beautiful rising sun on the horizon. Well, in theory he was looking at the spectacular sunrise. In practice, he was staring only at the enormous stack of papers on his desk inside his office. Petitions, aristocrat complaints, yesterday's articles on the coronation…but not today's paper. Why?

His thoughts drifted away from that tiny dilemma as the door of his office creaked open.

Footsteps traveled towards the balcony. Oh, *finally*, some mint tea and biscuits—

"More files for you, my prince," Advisor Lai's voice declared. And magically, more papers appeared on Urumi's desk. It was like Lai was the fairy godfather of mystical papers. (It would be nice if the papers were magical enough to do themselves, though.)

Urumi frowned. "Whatever could people be so uneasy about?"

Advisor Lai gave him the kind of glance that made him feel like an incompetent child. It was then followed by a factual update lecture.

"Poverty levels rising in the Southern Province, protests raging in the Western Province, ships sinking in the Eastern Province, bounty prices on your head, and…"

"Time gaps," he completed. Urumi twisted his brow as a maid came in with his tea. He took a massive sip before continuing. "Have one of our data and statistics collectors get an update on the exact poverty level rise in the Southern Province. Find the blueprints from the ships that have sunk and organize a meeting with the palace naval architects. We're going to need the information and addresses of the families of those killed in the naval disasters. Get Lady Jea to contact the families—"

"I'm afraid that won't be possible."

"Is she still on her trip to the Western Province?"

"No, my prince. She is no longer with us."

Urumi nearly spit out his tea. "What?!" Breathe. "Why, Lai?"

"Irrelevant, your majesty."

Irrelevant? How could death be irrelevant? Uh, he was getting sidetracked. This would be dealt with later when his mind wasn't jumping in circles just to get a word out.

"Continuing," he finally said. "For the protests in the Western Province, I'd like to arrange a live meeting with the public so that I can assure them—"

"Absolutely not, my prince," Advisor Lai said. "Just you being outside on this palace balcony is considered a security risk. I suspect your guards will be here any minute to take you inside."

"We are not going to get anything done living in a bubble," he argued.

"We are not going to get anything done if you are dead, my Prince," Advisor Lai replied.

"Evidently," he replied, trying his best to tone down his infuriated sarcasm. "So, what do you suggest we do?"

"Send the national security advisor to talk to the public."

"National security advisor?" he repeated. "Sending *the military* shall accomplish the same task. The public will see it as an act of oppression and become even more violent."

"Speaking of the military." Lai sighed. "Another one of Valaztein's military ships has docked on Tashikian soil."

"How many soldiers came with it?"

"Two hundred and four. Queen Miranda has trackers on all of them except for two that went rogue and disappeared into the Southern Province a few days ago."

Urumi inhaled, trying not to focus on his indisputable headache. "I'd like to consult with Queen Miranda in person," he said.

"I'm afraid that would not be advised in terms of safety," Lai replied.

"Why? What plausible evidence do we have of Dark magic in her kingdom? Rumors? Conspiracy theories?"

"Rumors approved by the TNDD."

"What does the Tashikian National Detective Department have to do with any of this? She is just a fellow ruler like me," he said.

"If you are a dictator, then yes, you two are very alike."

Urumi grabbed a biscuit. "Point taken."

"We need investors for the infrastructural reconstruction plan," Lai said. "I suggest King Wrengoff of Brindim."

"Absolutely not," Urumi replied. "How old was his wife Crystal when he married her? Fourteen?"

"Thirteen, my prince. However, if you cross out every possible investor because of moral standards, you are not going to have very much to stand on." Lai sighed as he got out his leather notebook and started scribbling. "Write a letter to the palace naval architects about your initiatives before your meeting with the national magic crisis advisor. I'll get the family contacts and brief one of the data and statistics collectors about the poverty level rise. Anything more?"

"No. Thank you, Lai." There was much, *much* more, but he didn't want to contemplate anything else. Lai shut the door and strolled inside. Just as expected, a few minutes afterward, the palace guards came outside to escort him back to his room.

"My Prince, you must come inside," they said.

Urumi sighed and picked up his abnormally tall stack of papers, not at all content to know that more stacks of papers of the same size waited for him in his office. Urumi followed the guards out the door and into his office, preparing himself for another very long day.

The palace archives were a favorite pastime of Urumi. Mostly because they were spacious and quiet, but he also liked to pass through the millions of boxes full of letters and mandates of the past rulers. It was almost like his way of compensating for the history lessons he no longer had the time to take. To think he had complained about them so often.

Today, he walked over to a box full of mandates from the past kings and queens of Tashiki. He pulled out a long piece of parchment paper, which he could immediately tell wasn't very old because of the paper's texture. Actually, most of the mandates and letters in the palace were from the past three rulers. The older documents were highly protected.

The moment he started reading the mandate, his jaw fell open, and his body was filled with an eerie disbelief.

❂

"Lai, what the hell is this?" Urumi yelled as he shoved the paper in his advisor's face a few minutes later.

Lai rubbed his hands through his wispy brown beard. "What?"

"Let me clarify," Urumi said as he read the paper. "This is the king writing: *This official mandate states that all passing from the Southern Province to other provinces is strictly prohibited as an act by this kingdom's sovereign. With the help of many international, magic-conscious, and health advisors, I have decided that separating the Southern Province from the rest of Tashiki will be the best way to ensure that the time gaps will not spread throughout the rest of the country. This is a private mandate and any press that leaks this information to the public will be immediately punished by the king. Signed, King Jiko.*"

"I've never seen any of this," Lai replied, with a look on his face that was just as suspicious as Urumi's look had been. "Because it is not in your father's handwriting."

The next few weeks, his entire staff was acting strange. A maid too insistent to get him whatever he wanted, a kitchen who was preparing all of his favorite dishes. And every question that he asked, Lai met with a biting of his tongue and a quick answer. All his meetings seemed to be strained, no matter how simple the actual topic of the discussion was. It was as if the kitchen and maids were consoling him for something that had not yet happened, and his advisors were keeping that same news from him.

Finally, he exploded.

It happened on a Tuesday, when he was suffering through another long, boring meeting with the incompetent press secretary. It seemed that yet again the press secretary, Demeire Kothan, had succumbed to the thickheaded will of the journalists. This meant that he only nodded to everything the press said, and whenever confronted with a difficult question just turned red and said "okay."

What was wrong with his staff?

"Good day, my prince," Kothan mumbled, and Urumi could sense a kind of unspoken tension.

"Good morning, Mr. Kothan," Urumi replied.

Kothan burst into a fumble of quickly paced words. "If you're going to fire me, I'd like to say that I understand why. With everything you have on your hands, I mean, the time gaps disaster and all. It's so—"

"Excuse me," Urumi interrupted. "What?!"

"Oh, I forgot." The press secretary covered his mouth, quivering.

"What?" Urumi asked.

Kothan wouldn't move, just shook his head like a terrified seven-year-old. Oh gosh, was he crying? This couldn't be happening… Not today. "Mr. Kothan. I shall repeat this once more," Urumi finished, his words quick, whispered, and sharp. "What is going on in this palace?"

Kothan opened his mouth. "Advisor Lai hasn't told you."

"Told me what?" Why was he being kept in the dark? He was going to be *king* for crying out loud! He could not lead his people without knowing why he was leading them! The door creaked open, and Lai stepped inside the room. He addressed him and the press secretary.

"Prince Urumi, Press Secretary Kothan," he began. "I'm going to take the prince for a moment. I believe we have some matters to discuss."

They had matters to discuss indeed.

Urumi stood in a chamber that he had never entered before. There seemed to be endless parts of the palace that were empty and unseen. The massiveness of the castle was completely unnecessary. Anyway, the room had only a few fire lanterns clinging to the peach-colored walls, which made for overall dim lighting. Lai was sitting in a beautiful mahogany wood chair, lined with pure silver, and Urumi sat in a similar chair.

"What did you have to discuss with me?" he asked.

Lai shifted in his chair. "It's about the time gaps," his advisor replied, clearly avoiding the question.

"I figured." Urumi bit his lip, a habit that Lai had always pressured him to break. The day his father had come back from the kitchen wine storage for the first time, Urumi had bit it so hard his lip began to bleed.

"Urumi, there's no way to say this lightly."

"What is it?" he pushed. "More people dead in the Southern Province? More time gap protests?"

"Urumi," Lai said. "It's so much worse than that."

"Lai, please. You have to tell me the truth."

Lai sighed. "Urumi. It's not just in the Southern Province. The time gaps are spreading. Everywhere."

Chapter 13: The White Joker and the Black Queen - (Ez)

```
Shagra: Eastern Province, Tashiki
```

Ez wondered about how dreams create interesting realities. For kids, they make the world brighter, as if all the things that could never be accomplished on Earth were possible someplace else. When he was little, sleep was an escape from the streets of Milu. He was always running, sprinting… trying to find a way out. Back then, there was still a voice in his head telling him to search for the realities he encountered in his dreams. Now, that voice was long gone and so were the happy dreams that came with it. Most days he couldn't sleep, and on those rare days where he would restlessly doze off, his dreams had lost all their majesty. Like what was happening now:

A girl ran from a million guards through the chambers of a crumbling palace. The walls were full of notes.

There must be something better in the next world.
I love you.
Death is only the next stage in life.
I'll see you again.

Goodbye.

They were the last words of the dead, and the stones they were engraved on fell to the floor like glass, shattered into a million pieces. Distant voices echoed in the halls... yelling, shrieking, wailing at the living who had forgotten them. But all the while, the girl ran.

The girl with thick black hair that cascaded down her shoulders in a tangled mess.

The girl who ignored everything around her and kept running.

Ez chased after her, somehow unnoticed by the guards that charged through the palace. Dozens of rooms flew by, and no one stopped running. The girl who was fighting for her life at the front of the crowd looked so familiar, but yet... he couldn't place her. All he could see was her back. The back of the girl who ran.

The girl that shot shadows from the palms of her hands.

The girl who knew the halls of her persecution far too well.

Finally, the whirlwind of dashing people halted. The girl opened the doors to a room and walked around as if she could trick time. But it was a dream. And the dream allowed for anything to happen. Yes, anything could happen to this girl who had stopped running. She passed a thousand weapons of torture, all the while muttering: "Miranda." But then she came to a mirror and fell to the floor. Ez could tell it was a mirror, but the guards blocked his view of the girl's face.

The girl who wept as she gazed into the surface of the mirror.

The girl who he knew meant the world to him, but that he still didn't remember.

The girl whose emerald green eyes shot daggers at him when she turned around.

The girl who yelled at him, "Liar."

Then, a woman seen only in shadow appeared, and the world fell into darkness and pain.

Ez woke up to a splash of freezing water slamming into his face.

"Wake up, Ez!"

Ariah smacked his arm with one hand and had the other one curled up in a fist beside her leg.

"It's 11 a.m.," Daunt's voice said from a brown chair across the room. That was when Ez got his bearings. He was lying on a bed in a crappy motel room somewhere in the Eastern Province of Tashiki. Daunt was bored and Ariah was frustrated because he had overslept. Whoa, he hadn't done that since... Uh, never mind. The important thing was that he was supposed to be in the town center of Shagra searching for the dragon heir. Back in Kry, some black-market dealer had given them a clue. Their conversation had gone something like this:

"Have you seen anything strange around here?" Ez had asked.

The man scoffed. "Have you seen anything normal around here?"

Ez and Ariah had turned to each other, certain that they weren't going to get any information this way.

"We're part of the Tashikian and Valezteinian Dragon Control Center," Ariah told him.

"We need to know if you saw any rogue Changelings here."

The guy just rolled his eyes and laughed. "Look, I know that you people aren't from around here, but you'd have to be a fool to believe that lie you just told me. Dragon Control Center? Nah, that sounds too legit for the late King Idiot. What are you really doing here?" So, he told a lie a little closer to the truth.

"We're spies for the queen of Valaztein," he said. "But we do need to know about the Changelings."

Satisfied, the man said, "Well, no soul in this town has ever seen a dragon, so you should go search someplace else."

"Alright, have you seen anyone leave the province recently?" he asked.

"Sure I have." The man pulled back his black hood, revealing crimson gashes on his pale skin. He glared at both of them. "But no information comes cheap in Kry. Especially for foreigners."

As quick as lightning, Ariah pulled a knife up to his chin. "Your country might have been falling apart for a decade or so, but mine's been at war for millennia. One thing I'm not foreign to is men in dark hoods trying to get paid moments before they die. Don't be that guy."

"Fine," the man said, but Ariah didn't move her knife. "A squad of thieves. Nothing interesting about them except that they were traveling with a foreigner."

Ez scowled. "Real specific. Care to elaborate or should my partner let her knife talk instead?"

The man's eyes flashed in fear, a look Ez had seen too many times. "The foreigner, she had light brown skin, too dark for these parts. And bright green eyes."

Ez held in a gasp. Naomi? Her dad was a Changeling. Could that mean...

"Names of the thieves," Ariah asked. The man quivered but didn't respond.

"I can't say—"

"Names, now!" After a few seconds, Ariah slashed his neck. It wouldn't kill him, but the scar sure wouldn't be pretty.

"Grek Queen and a girl named Amethyst."

Queen... where had he heard that name before? Anyhow, the man clearly didn't know anything else about the dragon heir's location, so Ariah and Ez went to the club the man was talking about. It was a dim-lighted, crowded location full of men shooting daggers with bad aim, betting on unlikely winners, and shoving their faces with shots. There, they learned that no one had seen Grek Queen or Amethyst for days. They'd made it through the ridiculously expensive passage to the Eastern Province without a dime in their pockets. How? Not a soul knew.

Anyway, back in the Eastern Province, Ez leaped out of bed, suddenly remembering his dream. It was Naomi. The girl with dark black hair and green eyes was Naomi! But why was his dream about her? Why wasn't he having nightmares about dragon massacres or his own torture at the hands of Miranda? Maybe it was a...

No. That would be insane. He wasn't even supposed to be thinking about Naomi in the first place. There were thousands of other people who could be the dragon heir. Unfortunately, this stupid dream was the only thing in his head as he walked toward the closet and gathered his things. But... was there really a problem with having a little safety net?

Of course not. He could get an agent that he knew to track, find, and watch Naomi. Actually, he had the perfect excuse. Sure, there were some rumors about him and Ariah fleeing the country without permission, but he still had an agent who owed him a favor. Besides, he could say that Miranda wanted any information gathered while watching Naomi to be directly reported to Ez. It was perfect.

Besides... what if she was the heir? The amulet kept pulling them in her direction.

So, he proposed a change of plans to Daunt and Ariah. The agent he was looking for had a fancy masquerade ball in Donim with the Tashikian ambassador who needed to speak with Miranda about the military ships docking on Tashiki's coast. (Yeah, the ones he and Ariah had run away on.) This agent's job was to make sure the ambassadors never got to Valaztein, and Zyon was very, very good at his job. And it didn't seem strange to Daunt or Ariah when Ez decided they should go to Donim and see if the dragon heir would go to a busier city.

They all arrived at the hotel exhausted, and Daunt and Ariah were sound asleep by ten. Ez waited one more hour just to make sure. All it would take was one quick shop at a costume store for his masquerade disguise, and no one would even know he was there. So, he tiptoed out of bed in the pitch-black dark, hoping that he wouldn't trip and wake someone up. He was so close to the door. Just a few more steps and—

"Hi, Ez," Ariah said. She appeared from the shadows in a raven-colored suit with puffed shoulders and a black crown atop her afro. She even had her voice modifier on, and her dark stiletto boots made a steady noise as she walked towards him, like the sound of a dagger drilling its way through someone's skill. At least, that was the idea. It was Ariah's Black Queen outfit.

Both she and Ez had been given disguises that would hide their true identities from the public of Valaztein. So basically, they weren't only Miranda's minions, they were also her costumed game pieces.

"Why are you wearing that?" he whispered.

She passed him a box that held a white suit. It was his White Joker disguise. "Here's the only way you're getting into that masquerade," Ariah said, also in a low voice. "I'm assuming that's where you're headed, correct?"

Ez sighed. He often forgot the insanity of the person he held in close company. Of course Ariah was in on his plan. "How did you know?" he asked.

"You still have the same night habits from when you were at Miranda's."

"What does that mean?" he murmured.

Ariah opened the door and they both stood in the hotel hallway. It was nice to be able to talk normally again.

"You whisper Naomi's name in your sleep," Ariah said. "And you aren't the only one who knows about Zyon's masquerade mission. You trust him, and you're scared Naomi isn't safe. I connected the dots."

"Fine. You know about it now. Go back to sleep." He tried walking away, but Ariah turned around and stopped him.

"Hold on, Ez. That party is only for selected guests. You can't just wear some cheap costume and expect they'll let you in. This suit is the only thing that's going to get you in without a proper invite."

He gave it back to her. "Take your stupid suit. I don't want anything to do with it."

He hated that suit. He hated it. It was like every piece he hated about himself was stitched into a costume. And the worst part was that he wasn't even himself when he wore it; he was just Miranda's puppet.

"This isn't about sentiments," Ariah told him. "It's just a piece of cloth."

"Fine," he said with gritted teeth. "But what are we going to do about Daunt if there's no one to watch him?"

"We'll be back before 3 a.m. He won't be awake."

So Ez became the White Joker for one last time, pointy shoes and all. But his voice modifier and his jingling joker hat that tinkled death's tune were tied for worst place. With that, he set off across the streets of a crumbling country with the woman who murdered his entire race following him to a party full of murderers and the about-to-be-murdered. There, he hoped to strike a deal with an agent who could send him back to a genocidal queen about the rebel princess he stabbed in the back. Oh, and he forgot to mention: the agent was fourteen and his entire face was covered in scars.

Ez and Ariah walked along the limestone pathway that stood right beside the harbor. Even at midnight, there were ships docking and supplies moving in the Eastern Province as the indigo waves crashed against the shoreline. A trail of bright orange floor lanterns blazed a path in the dark, and for a few moments, Ez was right back in the good old times.

He had everything: a beaming moon in the shadowy distance, a secret mission to destroy the Queen of Valeztein, and his best friend right by his side. Well, that last part was kind of screwed up, but for these few moments, he could pretend that everything was just as it should be.

He could pretend that the people who walked by them weren't terrified by their suits.

He could pretend that a mass murderer wasn't the closest thing he had to a friend this night.

And he could pretend that he hadn't messed up his entire life.

"Wanna stop for CrunchBars?" Ariah asked as she walked over to an old woman in a little cart with sparkling firelights selling crispy delights in bars. It was an old joke between them. Every time they saw an opportunity to get CrunchBars, they had to take it. Partially because it was the only thing they could find at a refill store after starving in the mountains for three days. Ever since, nothing had ever tasted better.

"Why not? We've got time to kill," Ez said even though he could tell that the woman was not exactly thrilled to have the White Joker and the Black Queen come for CrunchBars. Luckily, they got to the cart before she could roll it away to the main city blocks that were still in eyesight.

"What would you like?" the old woman quivered, fidgeting with her navy dress.

Ariah smiled as she ordered. "Caramel Taffy Ooze for me and a Lemon Poppyseed for the man right next to me." Wow, she remembered.

The woman handed them the CrunchBars and rolled away with her cart, but Ez managed to slip her a few dellum to pay for the bars. He might look like Miranda's evil minion, but he wasn't anymore.

"Thanks for the idea," Ez said. "And for remembering."

"What? That we have a pact to devour something from every CrunchBars cart in the world or that your favorite flavor is Lemon Poppyseed?"

He laughed. "I guess some things don't change in two years."

"I guess not," Ariah chuckled, already on a bench taking off her black stiletto boots.

"What are you doing?"

"It's at least ten minutes more to that party, and I don't feel like being in pain until I absolutely need to be."

Ez sat down on the bench with her, facing the ocean. "I know! I can barely feel my feet in these pointed monstrosities." He stared down at his shoes.

Ariah shook her head. "You think you've got it bad? Try sneaking in some place without these horrible heels sounding off."

"Have you met my hat? It has bells on it!"

Ariah looked up at the crown in her hair as she got up from the bench. "And don't even get me started on this crown. At least your hair is straight! Do you have any idea how hard it is to get this crown untangled from my curly hair?"

Ez smirked and continued walking along the limestone path. "Well, at least your suit's black. You don't have to worry about stains."

"Yeah," Ariah said. "It must be impossible to get bloodstains off of your suit."

Ez halted. His heart started racing a million times faster than it should as he thought about what Ariah said. Every day. That was how often he had had to get bloodstains off of his suit back with Miranda.

"I think we should really pick up the pace and stop wasting time talking," he said. The sound of the waves crashing almost covered the sound of his footsteps as he walked away.

"I'm sorry!" Ariah called after him.

"No, I'm sorry," Ez said. "For leading you to think that we could be friends. If the way I act made you feel like things could go back to the way they were, they can't."

Ariah's face fell, but she quickly brought it back up with a stern smirk. He knew that face. It was Ariah's often-used way of hiding pain through destruction.

"You're right. You're Ez Shores, and you don't need anyone in your life. Well, I'm glad I can help in letting you die alone!" She charged ahead of him. Uh! She had no right to do that. She was the one in the wrong.

"I'm going to die alone?" he snapped back at her. "You murdered your own mother!"

She slapped him. "To save you, idiot!"

"You think that's what I would have wanted?!"

Ariah plastered on a fake smile. "Oh no." She finished off her statement with a deadpan. "I thought you would have wanted YOUR HEAD NAILED TO A WALL!"

He curled up his fists. "I've been in jail plenty of times before. Why didn't you think I'd get out?"

"Are you stupid?" Ariah screamed. "I made a deal with Miranda to let you out. Without me, you never would have made it out alive."

"Well, maybe I'd rather be dead than a traitor!"

Ariah lowered her voice. They had arrived at the gates to the mansion where the masquerade ball was being held.

"Look at you," she said. "Such a hero. Wait no, that's your girlfriend who you betrayed."

"Don't talk to me about betrayals," he snarled.

Ariah didn't even care to sneer back at him. All she said was: "We're both traitors, Ez, and sooner or later our kill counts will round to the same number. The only difference is: I've accepted what I am. When are you going to?"

And with those words in his head, Ez walked into the masquerade ball with a fake grin.

He had never been more grateful that few people wanted to talk to the White Joker.

Ariah had been right about the suits. The man holding the invite list didn't even look at them as they strolled inside the party, and my, was it a party.

Hundreds of people gathered in a giant room where a ten-foot diamond chandelier stretched across the enormous glass ceiling through which you could see the vibrant night sky. Clearly that was the theme of the party, because silver stars detailed the marble walls, and servants ran up and down the two magnificent stairways with chocolate planets. People played all sorts of games over dozens of crystal tables. The money limit? There was none. And Ez knew exactly where he would find Zyon, fooling around with the rich.

"Good evening, Zyon," Ez said as Zyon wowed everyone with a royal flush. Sure, Zyon was fourteen, but he was pretty tall for his age, and everyone at the table knew better than to turn down one of Miranda's agents for a round of poker. Zyon had a full-face mask, just like Ez's. However, he had traded in his usual slick black for a cerulean blue. He wore a gold and sapphire suit that Ez knew was made by Miranda's special designer. The rose in his top pocket was perfect and shiny, dripping with luminous stardust poison that was undetectable to the untrained eye. His mask had an elisium backing so that no one could reveal his identity; elisium was practically unbreakable. Zyon had even replaced the usual cards in the deck with special ones that could turn into any card he desired. It was a nice touch, but the black edges gave them away to someone like Ez.

"Good evening, Joker," Zyon said in an upscale accent. Then, he saw Ariah coming up behind Ez. "Oh, you are both here. I'd imagine the matter is of utter importance." Wow, Zyon was really enjoying himself. Between the expensive suit, all the money he had stolen through his poker cheats, and the ridiculous accent, Ez could tell that Miranda didn't have a close eye on him. No way she would let an elite agent go gallivanting around like a child. Unless... he wasn't in use. Perfect.

"Yes, it is important," Ariah told him.

"So I don't suppose you have a few minutes for a round of poker?"

Ez shook his head. "We need to speak to you privately."

Zyon led them up the extravagant marble staircases to chambers in the mansion where they certainly were not supposed to be. On the way, Zyon handed the rose to a woman in a navy silk dress, grinning flirtatiously. Then, he led them to a small room with a long wooden conference table and dozens of bookshelves where they sat down to talk.

"Why are you here?" Zyon said, losing his fake accent in a second.

"We rank above you, Zyon," Ariah snapped. "We ask the questions."

Zyon cracked his knuckles and grinned. "Unless you went rogue. I've heard some rumors about you fleeing Valaztein."

"Well, those rumors are wrong," Ez said. "We're on an off-the-grid mission for Miranda."

"What about?"

"You'll know soon enough," Ariah responded. "For now, we have a mission for you. Track down Naomi Elistaire. Everything you find gets reported directly to us. Not Miranda."

Zyon scoffed. "And what makes you think I'd do that?"

Ez stared him straight in the eyes. Zyon was playing games with them, but everyone in that room had a crystal-clear idea of which people had the power.

"You owe me a favor," Ez said. "A big one. I don't care about why you think we're here. All I know is that if you turn us in, I'm sure Miranda would love to know the real reason your face is covered in scars."

Zyon gritted his teeth. "You swore—"

"And I intend to keep my promise. If it weren't for me, you would have died after your little escapade." It seemed cruel to use the worst day of Zyon's life as emotional blackmail. Ez could still see that little kid screaming in the palace fields, stabbed and half-dead. Zyon's attempt to escape Miranda almost cost him his life.

The intelligent decision would have been to leave him to die, but Ez had trained him. Besides, Zyon was *fourteen*. In what kind of cruel, twisted world would a fourteen-year-old be stabbed to death? Uh, he shouldn't answer that.

In the same kind of world in which little children were taken from their homes and trained to become assassins.

"I'll help you," Zyon said. "You helped me instead of tracking down Heather. I'll do whatever you need."

Ez sighed. "Thank you. All I need you to do is track down Naomi. Make sure that she stays out of harm's way and report her every action to me."

Zyon nodded, and as they all walked out of the room, sirens blared.

"The Tashikian ambassador has been murdered!" a woman screamed.

Ez could feel Zyon grinning through his mask. Of course, the lady to whom he gave the poisoned rose was the ambassador, but the poison would take a few minutes to kick in. Zyon was with Ez and Ariah, so he had the perfect excuse. Ez was disgusted by Miranda's solution to the problem of having an ambassador come over, but he couldn't help but feel a little proud.

He had trained Zyon, after all.

Chapter 14: Twisting Fate - (Amethyst)

```
Donim: Eastern Province, Tashiki
```

Fire. The world was on fire, or at least hers was. The inside of the once dark, damp cabin was now burning with light and heat. She waited for her lungs to make an adjustment to the fire, but they didn't. There was no relief; there was no oxygen. Only fire.

What the heck caused it? She replayed the night in her head and then remembered in a flash. Damn it... Grek and his disgusting cigarettes.

"Amethyst!" Naomi yelled from ahead of her. "Come on!"

Quickly, Amethyst had found that she had little-to-no things to relate to Naomi with, but apparently, both of them attracted danger with every step. Amethyst heard a faint creaking above her as she kept running, but didn't think much of it as she made her way through the flaming wooden cabin. When Naomi turned around to check on Amethyst, her face warped into one of grotesque surprise.

Naomi screamed something she couldn't hear, but there was no time to even look up before the piece of flaming wooden roof detached and fell right above her. All she felt was a harsh impact against her shoulder as Naomi threw herself against her, shielding Amethyst from the scorching flames with her shadows.

"Thank you," she said, breathless.

"No problem," Naomi responded. "Let's go." They continued making their way through the cabin, with nothing giving even the slightest hint of hope. The first sign of life she saw was a badly burned hand.

It was Grek's.

No, this couldn't be happening. They had come all this way to get enough money to start a better life, not to end their own lives.

"Grek!" she screamed. "Grek! Wake up!"

Nothing. He must've been unconscious. Naomi rushed over.

"Let's pull him out." They both grabbed his hand and gently pulled Grek out of the ashen mess of fire and wood to a safer area of the cabin, careful not to put him in the path of more flames. He looked fine. *Fine.* Of course, just a little burned around the edges. She'd make jokes about this later, right?

No. Not right. She was not okay with a "crispy" version of her best friend, and she was about to have a heart attack. Naomi gave her a pat on the back and walked away in search of the rest of their team.

"I found Heather and Miko!" Naomi shouted from a few feet away. Miko was jumping up and down. The snow monkey was conscious and as ready as ever. Heather, on the other hand, was in between consciousness and unconsciousness.

"Naomi…" she muttered. "Where…"

"The cabin is on fire."

Heather shook her head, gazing up at a hole in the cabin's roof. "Then why are they here?"

Amethyst watched as Naomi focused on that hole. Two men peered down at them. One had slick raven-black hair and ice-blue eyes. The other man had a black mask covering up his entire face, and his hair was cut razor short. But they were gone in a flash.

"Ez," Naomi mumbled.

"Zyon..." Heather gasped.

Amethyst didn't pay much attention to either of them. She was tired and worn out; the men could be figures of her imagination. *Then why did Heather and Naomi see them, too?* she thought. Ah, whatever, she had bigger problems.

Like the fact that her best friend was unconscious in a burning cabin.

As Naomi took care of Heather, Amethyst channeled all her focus into waking Grek.

"Grek. Wake up!"

She slapped him on the cheek.

Hard.

Still nothing. After a ten-time repeat, all Grek gave was a groan. Oh well, at least he was awake.

"Go away," he mumbled.

Oh, so he just didn't *feel* like waking up?

"Your chest is on fire!" she lied. Nothing. "I'm joining the Brindimic Skondivan, and you'll be my live sacrifice." Nothing. Finally, it went down to the unchallenged solution that always woke Grek up. "Your hair's a blob."

Grek sprang to his feet and screamed. He gave Amethyst the death stare as he touched his hair (which was still frustratingly perfect, although a bit burned). Grek must also have noticed his surroundings because a stream of cusses sprung from his mouth like a slick river.

"Grek!" Heather yelled from the other side of the room. Naomi, Heather, and Miko rushed towards Amethyst and Grek. But as they reached them, Amethyst saw a glint of burning fire out of the corner of her eye.

"WATCH OUT!" Naomi shrieked.

A chunk of the ceiling had dispatched, leaving them blocked off from the only possible exit.

Naomi began lifting her hand. It was to use her awful shadow magic thing, Amethyst guessed, but Grek stopped her.

"Wait," he said. "Amethyst, you can fix this, right?"

She blinked. "Huh?"

"You can fix this. I know you can," Grek repeated.

"Grek, my powers only work like thirty percent of the time," she responded. "I don't think I can—"

"What powers?" Heather blurted out. She stared at Grek. Grek stared back.

"Um…" Amethyst started, but before she could finish, another one of the stabilizing wooden poles crashed to the ground, and they all bolted out of the way.

"Whatever your powers are, try it!" Naomi yelled from the other side of the room. "I'll cover you!"

Naomi lifted her hands and poured out shadows, but Amethyst closed her eyes before she could see what happened next.

Rewind.

Focusing on the clock, she skipped to the last step of her process; it would save her a lot of time. A lot of time they didn't have. But of course, her mind loved to spend time on useless thoughts. Like her vision. Somehow, that was all she could think of as the clock in her mind ticked back in time.

Backwards.

Twenty, nineteen, eighteen, seventeen, sixteen, fifteen, fourteen...... Who was the second figure?

Stop thinking.

Why could Miri mold shadows?

Why could Naomi mold those very same shadows with a gold tint?

Thirteen, twelve, eleven, ten, nine.......

Where had King Jiko taken the baby?

This is wasting time.

Who sent her the visions?

Why did they always happen after she used her powers?

Eight, seven, six...

Did Grek's pattern mean anything?

Stop it.

Why did she have powers?

Why did she get visions?

Five, four...

What had happened during the first three years of her life?

Shut up.

Why was Heather alive?

Three, two...

Who the hell was the dragon heir?

One.

The clock was spinning now, but forward and way too fast. She couldn't stop it; she couldn't control it. No, no, no, no, no, no! She fought it with her mind, with her pure will, but the clock didn't even slow. Whatever controlled her powers wanted her to see something in the future, but the future was something she had promised never to tamper with.

"KNOCK ME OUT!" she cried at the top of her lungs, hoping that someone would hear and stop her disaster. She imagined all of them confused, except for Grek.

Thank heavens for Grek. And sure enough, the hit to the head that knocked her out came from Grek and Grek alone. She sighed and hoped that she would wake up in time to help them. Then, Amethyst realized that she had bigger problems, because the moment she hit the hard floor, a vision began to kick in.

It was the same old process, except everything was at superspeed. Drowning, flipping, falling, the bridge, it all seemed to happen in the same millisecond. Falling from the bridge was just as quick as everything else, and though she knew it wasn't real, it all left Amethyst wanting to throw up.

When she landed, Amethyst tried to get her bearings but failed. Miserably. This was because the ground and the walls and the ceiling were blank. Literally blank. They weren't white, no. It was more like a weightless, airy, blank void. Her visions did this when they didn't want her to see something, or better said: know something.

Sometimes she wondered if a person was controlling her visions. Whoa, that would be strange.

In her vision, a man walked into the room, begging. Oh, it was Grek. He was on his knees now. Why was he doing that? Her stomach did a flip, uneasy. Her unease only grew when the figure attacking him was revealed. It was her, Amethyst.

What?

No. No. It couldn't be right. She would never threaten Grek. She would never hurt *Grek.*

She closed her eyes, but it didn't matter. She would still have to see everything, because the vision was in her head. A crushing headache rushed through her skull, and breathing became anywhere from difficult to impossible.

This was not real. This was not real. It hadn't happened yet. It hadn't happened yet.

But it would.

She shrieked, but it was only in her vision, so no one could hear. She screamed again, knowing that it would do nothing.

Her scream was parallel with Grek's, because the Amethyst in her vision had pulled out a knife and plunged it into Grek's lower stomach.

No.

Amethyst in the vision lifted up the knife and plunged it at Grek's upper stomach.

"Stop!" Real Amethyst yelled, sobbing into her shirt. "Stop it! Stop!" As the cruel, twisted Amethyst in her vision plunged the knife at Grek's shoulder, she ran up to him in her vision, knowing that she could do nothing. If the future appeared in her visions, it was just as set in stone as her past.

The Amethyst in her vision had blood soaking her hands and all through her arms up to her shoulders. Grek was screaming.

Stop!

Nothing. The world would not stop for her wishes and neither would fate.

Please.

The knife plunged into Grek's heart.

"You're not my best friend," he said, and Amethyst was sure he said a name but the vision beeped to cover it. A single tear streamed down his face as the life went out of the only person who had ever cared if she lived or died. "Tell Analuna I love her." Amethyst, the real Amethyst, could just see the last flicker of light go out of him in the blurry fog of her tears. And a voice in her mind whispered: *Without Grek, you're worthless. You've always been worthless.*

The vision stopped, and she woke up, not caring to analyze her surroundings.

Because Grek would die.

She would kill him.

And the one consistent thing about her visions: they always, absolutely always came true.

Chapter 15: Loops of Time - (Ez)

```
Eastern Province, Tashiki
```

Ez followed Zyon into a dark forest, Ariah and Daunt trailing him. The sky was nearly pitch black and the trees were so close together that three steps in the wrong direction could lead someone astray. Zyon had found the cabin where Naomi was staying, and Daunt had begged to come.

But the most surprising thing: Ez had let him!

Ez hoped he didn't have any kids. What a great parent he'd be to let a kid run out into the woods to chase someone down.

They reached a clearing in a forest.

"Go through those trees right there and you'll find where they're staying," Zyon said.

Ez, Ariah, Zyon, and Daunt walked around a little pond onto a slim path between dozens of pearly white trees that held a slight glimmer in the dusky night. Did he smell... smoke? At first, he figured that it came from a campfire that Naomi had created, but it was a completely different matter indeed.

An entire wooden cabin was on fire.

His heartbeat raced at the speed of lightning. What if Naomi was in the cabin? He climbed up the wall of the cabin, searching for the spots that were untouched by flames. In the corner of his eye, Ez caught a glimpse of Zyon, who stood next to him.

And then he saw Naomi. She was running through the flames, searching for something or someone. A girl ran up behind her with black and white stripes of hair wrapped into a messy bun at the top of her head. Her face was strangely familiar somehow, but Ez didn't dwell on it too much.

"Heather!" Naomi called.

Zyon and Ez snapped a glance at each other.

"Heather Queen?" Zyon asked, his expression darkening.

The girl with striped hair screamed in the flaming room. "Grek, wake up!" She was beside a man covered by planks of wood. This was it: their squad of thieves. The thought had barely crossed his mind; it would be so strange, so unlikely... Was Naomi the dragon heir? Could her ties to Nicholae make her the mythical beast from the verse?

Ariah called them from behind.

"Guys, come back to—"

The moment she started speaking, a sequence of events began to unfold.

The ground shook and a skull-crushing headache rammed through his head. The world itself seemed to break, sending them crashing to somewhere... something else. They were zooming through a white void, with time and space and every law of gravity gone.

Daunt screamed in the blankness.

Ariah gritted her teeth in pain.

A wave of energy slammed into Ez, Ariah, and Daunt.

Zyon dashed out of the way.

Ez's vision went blurry, and a giant claw scratched at him from inside.

His surroundings changed to a giant clock. They were climbing it now.... up, up, up, and yet going nowhere.

Ez lost sight of Ariah as he reached the top of the clock.

Daunt was behind him, clawing his way up. Just two more steps, but Daunt slippe—

Ez snatched Daunt in an unrelenting grasp.

"Ez, I'm scared!" Daunt shrieked, tears streaming down his face.

"Don't let go." Ez stared Daunt straight in the eyes. "Promise me you won't let go."

"I promise," he quivered.

"Close your eyes."

"Will it make a difference?" Daunt asked.

"I don't know."

Daunt did as he was told. Ez could only hope that he was right. He was standing on the outside of a giant cerulean and gold clock. From where Ez stood, he could see the second hand and the minute hand, but not the hour hand. Best guess, that was probably where he was standing. The clock was set at military time, but before he could observe anything more, the second hand lashed at him. This knocked him towards the black endless abyss that lay beneath the giant vertical clock, an abyss that he didn't want to fall into. Ez grabbed onto the second hand, checking to make sure Daunt hadn't fallen off too. No, he hadn't fallen, but he was screaming and crying from his perilous position on the edge of the hand.

"You have to jump!" Ez shouted.

"What?!"

"Jump!"

Daunt neared closer to the edge of the hand, breathing heavily. He mumbled something to himself, and whatever it was worked, because Daunt leaped from the hand. His jump was an inch too short, and if not for the number six, Daunt would've disappeared into the abyss. Ez launched himself at the little boy and managed to grab his hand. Thankfully, there was no coming short then, but as Ez touched six, something far worse happened.

Because he was six again. Somehow he was in his six-year-old body, staring at the three other people in that carriage.

No, no, no, no, no, no, no.

He could not watch himself do this. He could not relive this moment again.

His mother. Her eyes beaming with hope, her hands fidgeting with excitement, grabbing his.

"We're going to start a new life, darling. You might not understand why we're doing this now, but you will soon."

She was wrong. He understood what they were doing perfectly. Six-year-old Ez only had a messed-up sense of morality.

His knife touched her first. Then there was his father who said, *Please, stop this.*

His dad's outgoing smile was content and proud. Proud of his son. Proud of the monster he had created. The knife pierced him second.

This isn't fair. This isn't fair.

Why was he reliving the worst part of his life?

But there was still one person to go through before he could leave this cursed memory.

The last person in the car. The last person whom he couldn't kill. The last person whom he'd never be able to kill.

Once is enough.

Finally, it stopped. He was back on the clock, grabbing onto the minute hand, willing himself to keep it together. For Daunt. For Daunt, who hadn't yet come out of his horror. For Daunt, who never deserved this. For Daunt, who willingly entrusted his life to a murderer.

And as he searched for Daunt, Ez slipped.

His foot touched the eight by accident. This couldn't be happening.

He was with Ariah. They were exchanging the bracelets. The very same bracelets that were now shattered to pieces on the floor of the palace. They made an oath to be friends forever. That oath died long before the bracelets had.

He awoke on the second hand. Ez barely lasted two seconds before smacking his head on number sixteen. Wow, there was a large selection of painful memories on number sixteen.

But this memory was strange, because it was pleasant and peaceful and luring. He was in Milu... with Naomi. Unfortunately, there were three things that told him it was fake. First, Naomi seemed calm, not terrified like she had looked that day. Two, she referred to him as Ez, not Assassin Man. And three, well, three was probably the easiest to spot: she loved him.

"This isn't real," he told Fake Naomi, and partially himself.

"What do you mean, this isn't real, Ez?" Fake Naomi responded.

"You just called me Ez."

"So?" Fake Naomi replied. She moved closer to him. He wanted to lean in, but knew that it wouldn't do anything.

"You're not real," he rephrased.

"Of course I'm real," she said sweetly. Then her voice changed. Deeper, darker. It was not her voice. It was the Queen's. "I made this for you, Esmond. This is real. It's only a different version of real. Like a separate reality; a reality in which you never betrayed her."

He grimaced. "What are you doing in a time gap, Miranda?" And just like that, she was gone, replaced with Fake Naomi.

"I'm not Miranda." How was this possible? How could everything be so... real. The way her hands fidgeted. The way her eyes never seemed to lose their wonder. The way she smiled when he almost made her laugh. The black abyss from the clock appeared in the distance, and Naomi started running towards it.

"Come with me," she said. "We can be happy again."

Was it really so simple? Could he really just stay there forever? Such an easy solution to all his problems; to all his worries.

But Daunt—that poor little kid. Daunt deserved the world. He deserved the big house and the loving parents and the perfect childhood. Daunt was Ez's do-over, a way to fix all the mistakes in his short, painful life. Daunt deserved the life Ez never had.

If I can save this little kid, then maybe I'm not such a monster. And he would die before seeing Daunt's life turn into his.

And then there was Naomi. She was still alive, and he had to keep her that way.

"No," Ez said quietly, and then louder. "No! I can't go with you. I've gotta save you, Princess. And I know you'll hate me for it."

The image dispersed, and Fake Naomi pixelated into a thousand pieces, taken out of reality just as he knew she would be.

Ez sighed. He was back on the hour hand with Daunt, who was crying into his shoulder.

"Come on, Daunt," he said. "Let's go get Ariah." Ez wondered what Daunt had seen in his vision, because he just nodded, quiet for the first time ever.

Ariah dangled from the eight, smiling. She looked so happy. It was almost cruel of him to break her from the trance.

"Ariah!" he shouted.

"Oh, Ez," she replied, as if she meant to be dangling.

"Wait there!" he said. "I'll help you out."

"Ez, that really won't be necessary."

"What?"

He could see her hand slipping. He had to do something. He had to—

"I have to do this. Please."

No, she couldn't be doing this. There was so much left to say.

"You're just gonna leave us," he said, fear slowly turning to anger.

"I'm not—"

"You're weak!"

"I know!" she yelled. "But there's nothing left for me to do. Please. Let me do this."

"I haven't forgiven you. I never will. Not even in your grave."

But Ez thought for one moment that maybe... Maybe he could forgive her in the years to come, but he quickly remembered how ludicrous that really was.

And Ariah just nodded at his words, her grip on the number waning, tears streaming down her face. She gazed at the abyss. "But he will."

"Who?" Daunt asked, farther behind Ez.

Ariah looked at him. "You wouldn't believe it."

"Don't do this." Ez shook his head. "You don't have to do this."

"I do. You have Naomi and the dragon heir and even a little smidge of hope left. I don't."

"You have me."

Ariah gazed at him blankly.

"We all know who has you, Ez." A tear slipped down her cheek. Ez could see her reject her reflexes, swiping away the tear as if it were poison. "Even those of us who don't want to."

"Ariah..." Ez reached for her arm and desperately yanked her towards safety.

"Get off me!" she screamed. "Or I'll jump right now."

"Please, we're just kids. We've got our whole lives ahead—"

"Just kids?" Ariah sobbed. "I lost my childhood a long time ago, Ez."

"Don't let your life end at eighteen. Please." Why was she doing this? "We have our whole lives ahead of us, a lifetime of memories to fix all the screw-ups!" Ariah gave him a lopsided grin, her body trembling as her muscles began to give out.

"You really must love her."

"I love you," he lied.

"And all I had to do was die." Ariah chuckled. "Always have been a terrible liar, Ez."

He wanted to grasp her arm and throw her onto the safety of the clock. He wanted to yell and shriek until she pulled herself up. But none of it would help. She had made her decision.

Now, all that was left for him to do was accept it. "Goodbye, Ariah."

Then, in a voice so low Ez could barely hear, Ariah said, "*I* love you. You never will."

She let go of the number eight.

In her absence, time reset, and Ez was back in the forest with Daunt.

But all he could think of was Ariah. Why did they call her state "Lost"? Why that very impermanent word for something so very permanent?

Ariah was dead.

And if she was dead, then Ez knew that there was no point in his silent screaming, yelling out a long-broken promise.

Chapter 16: Timed Out on Whiskey Street - (Amethyst)

(Capital) Mae Lì: Northern Province, Tashiki

Amethyst trudged through the snowy streets of Mae Li, drowsy and restless. Between her own eyebags and her crispy-around-the-edges friends, she felt so out of place among the tall, elegant buildings and the delicate little plazas. Finely dressed strangers strolled along in their dainty petticoats and silky garments, probably on their way to pick up their children at school. She could almost feel her heart jump when a smiling dad swung his daughter around and then wrapped her up in an embrace.

Oh, what she'd give for that.

What she'd give to have someone to braid her hair into one of those neatly pinned buns she'd always thought were so stylish. To have someone to twirl her around like a princess in her lily-blue laced dress. But why was she even having such ridiculous thoughts? Parents like that aren't reserved for grimy thieves.

Besides, Amethyst had to focus. Back in that cabin… well, she couldn't fail her friends like that again. Uh, she was out of control! If it weren't for Naomi's shadow powers, they would've died in that cabin. Because of her.

Naomi's voice interrupted her little mind argument, because at least one person was thinking practically.

"We have to find the prince," she said. Grek turned around, the bags under his eyes very visible.

"Not tonight," he said. "I don't think any of us can stand another night without food and sleep."

Naomi looked around, her eyes softening as she saw her exhausted crew. Miko was literally sleeping on her shoulder, Grek and Heather were covered in ashes, and Amethyst herself could barely walk in a straight line. Walking reminders of all they'd been through to get here.

Of all they'd suffered for this faraway dream.

"You're right," Naomi replied. "Can you go buy us something to eat, Grek?"

Heather rolled her eyes. "With what money, Elistaire?"

"Oh, right."

Grek just grinned. "That's not a problem."

Turns out, it *was* a problem. This was because five hours later, it was nearly one a.m. and Grek was nowhere to be found. Thankfully, they had been able to get a night's stay at a hotel by doing a heinous number of chores. Naomi (who, of course, couldn't be seen by anyone because they might recognize her) had met Grek in the location they had decided upon, but he wasn't there. In the haze of city nightlife, it was impossible to find him. After searching all the places where he would most likely steal, Amethyst realized the nature of his little trip.

"Where could he be?" Heather asked.

Amethyst sighed. "Walk towards the flashing lights."

"What does that mean?"

"Clubs," Naomi answered. It was only a few more blocks to the most crowded streets, but it felt like an eternity. And sure enough, there he was, lounging on the corner of a street, wooing some pretty stranger.

How could he be so irresponsible!? They had crossed through the Southern Province illegally, were traveling with royalty and outlaws, and Grek still didn't understand how much was on the line!

Years and years of waiting in that dump had shown her that there was nothing she wouldn't do to get out. But she would've stayed if Grek wanted to. She would do anything for Grek, because he had always done the same for her.

So why'd he always come back to the flashing lights?

He began crossing the street towards her, nonchalantly strolling along a busy road without looking forward. That's when Amethyst saw the carriage racing right at him. Her body reacted before anything else could, sprinting forward and imagining a clock. She counted backward, praying that her powers would work with her. And somehow, the world reeled back, giving her five minutes. No vision this time; just the most valuable five minutes she would ever get.

So, she told Naomi and Heather to pick up the pace, because they were still a few blocks away after her little time shift. She settled into a steady run and caught Grek well before he crossed the street.

Finally, she was staring him straight in the eyes on the street corner, trying to forget all that had just happened.

"Amethyst," he said. "I'm sorry—"

"No." She wiped a tear from her eye. "You don't get to be sorry, okay? If you only knew how much danger you were in..."

"What are you saying?"

"I used my powers because you almost died," she told him. "So I'm not putting up with this anymore! You're family, the only one I've got, so you are never getting near any one of these clubs again. You have to promise me!"

She expected him to whine or protest like he usually did, but Grek didn't say a word for at least a minute. Instead, he hugged her so tight she could barely breathe.

"I promise."

And in that moment, she knew that she would never have the embrace that that little girl got from her dad, but it didn't matter, because she had this one.

Chapter 17: Some Things Are Best Left Unsaid - (Ez)

(Capital) Mae Lì: Northern Province, Tashiki

Ez tried to go on as if nothing had happened, but that was impossible. Ariah's death was the only thing on all of their minds as he, Zyon, and Daunt walked towards Mae Li. Daunt hummed an eerie tune, trying to hide the tears bubbling up in his eyes, while Zyon merely gazed out into the distance, wary. And Ez just tried to focus on anything else.

The scenery changed drastically as they approached Mae Li. Snow fell from lofty trees, and imposing buildings stood not too far from them. It reminded him of how Zurei had once been, before Naomi had gone into the Maze. He looked at the buildings differently now, though. Where he had once looked up, unaware of the cruelty and corruption taking place inside, now he looked down, wondering if he was any better than those crooked people.

Ariah would have said it was all pointless, but in the end, she was just as desperate for acceptance as anyone else. Still, he never could have imagined that it was his acceptance that she was searching for. Ariah's mind had always been uncrackable, and her drive as well. Ez had always thought nothing could break her, especially not her conscience.

But he was wrong. And somehow, the memories from before she had betrayed him, mixed with how utterly lost she had been recently made everything so much worse. Which Ariah was he supposed to remember? The brave, loyal friend who would do anything for him or the merciless traitor she had been all these years? Miranda's accomplice or just another pawn in the Queen's game?

None of it made any sense. Of course, he had dealt with loss, but how could he feel sorry for a person whose identity he never really knew?

"Ez, I'm freezing," Daunt said, interrupting his spiraling mind. Sure enough, Ez turned around to see him shivering.

"Take my jacket," Ez said, handing it to him. "I'm not that cold anyway." That was a lie, but Daunt had gone through enough for today.

"Are we going into the city?" Zyon asked.

"Best to just camp out here for today," Ez replied. The sun had just come up, and none of them had slept well after Ariah jumped, so it was best for them to rest. "I have some business to attend to in the city, but I'll be back before dinner."

This business was something he'd been meaning to do for a while. Back at the cabin, he'd dropped a miniature tracker on Naomi and on Heather Queen, who Zyon wanted to find. With their location known, he planned to drop off a letter for Naomi, explaining things.

As Zyon started setting things up, Daunt began chirping and chattering again.

"What business?" he asked.

"Not yours," Zyon snapped. So Ez headed on his way to the city, and as he walked, he remembered that he still had Miranda's diary in his satchel. The entries could be useless or full of secrets. Either way, it was eye-opening to read through the mind of someone as messed up as Miranda. Every word was another clue to the wiring of her brain, something he wasn't sure he would ever understand. So, Ez sat down on the roots of a barren tree to read another entry.

Dear Diary,

Good day. Today is the 21st of the month, which means today I have to visit the people.

They aren't the wealthy members of the court or the diplomats from other countries. No, these are real townspeople, and I hate every moment with them.

My father says that it's important to see how people live in your country, but I stopped listening to him a long time ago. Because I hate the way they look at me. Maybe my dad and his flashy new wife are content with the forced bows and fake smiles, but I can see through all of that. Deep in their eyes lies the anger, the hate, the jealousy. Today I saw a little boy, and no one had told him that those were emotions you have to hide.

So he spit in my face.

And, of course, the shadows didn't like that. In that moment, I was uncontrollable, an exact reflection of my outraged temper. A black hand materialized in front of me, and that shadow was around the boy's neck faster than I could control it. How dare he? *I was thinking in that moment. He judged me so easily, yet he had no idea how I suffered each night.*

And then I was being restrained by ten different guards. In a second, I had gone from untouchable royalty to a dangerous monster that had to be contained. All I thought of was my father. He just stood there, and I couldn't tell whether he was afraid or disappointed.

I hope he was afraid. I hope he was terrified of what he had created.

Sincerely,

Miri

Ez was shaken. How old could she have been in that letter? Thirteen? Fourteen? Of course, he'd had his share of childhood trauma, but none of his Changeling abilities had ever controlled him like that. Which made him think: did Naomi feel the same thing with her shadows?

And as he kept walking, Ez continued to think of his Changeling abilities. Oh, what he'd give to turn into a dragon right now. There was nothing like the wind brushing against his scales or the feeling of being so far above everything else. It would be so much faster too, but he couldn't screw everything up when he was this close. The dragon heir was somewhere in Mae Li; he was almost there! Ariah was gone, so he had never been more determined to find the only remaining link to his past.

An heir that could very well be Naomi herself. For that reason, Ez decided to stop at Mae Li's public archives before continuing to Naomi's hotel. Also, it provided a much-needed detour so that he could build up the strength to deliver the letter.

The archive was a tall white brick building with iron towers spiraling high into the clouds on each side. The frost coated them beautifully, making the whole library look like a snowy mountain with two glittering peaks.

Ez strolled through the ornate gold doors (an unsurprising waste of money for a country almost more classist than Valaztein) and wondered why hadn't done more research on the dragon heir before fleeing the country on a wild rabbit chase. It could be anything! A person, a dragon, a Changeling... how far did the dragon bloodline have to go?

Could a regular person be the dragon heir if they had some kind of ties to dragon blood?

Someone like Naomi?

He flipped through book after book after book, scouring the lavish wings of the library for any signs of the dragon heir. Why hadn't he considered that it might be nearly impossible to find information on one of the rarest creatures in dragon mythology in a country where dragons don't exist?

Finally, Ez found it. On the last floor of the east tower, he encountered a massive textbook. Gold trim surrounded the pages and odd patterns were embroidered on the cover, almost like incantations. He blew the dust off the cover and flipped through the book. It seemed to be written in... Old Tongue? He hadn't read a book in old dragon tongue since, well, since the massacre.

In the days of Xakro, when spirits roamed the land and great kings of scales ruled the Earth, the rumblings began. Mahre Aya (Mother Sun, Ez knew) *sent signs with the seasons, scorching the land in her distress.*

Chakra Lani (a famous fatereader in dragon history) *knew the Golden Age of peace would come to an end one day. Aya warned that the world as the dragons knew it would die. Queen Alani, wife to the Great Xakro, was prepared to make the ultimate sacrifice to ensure the continuation of her race.*

Blood for blood.
Bone for bone.
Life for life.

As Alani had already lived half a life, it was said that the dragon heir would receive half of Alani's blood and half of another's. The dragon race's true savior.

"Mahre Aya, I give my life to the heir of my people. Send them to this world when we need it most. Let the magic that runs in their veins bring back our people. Let their blood of gold bring life to the New World. Herare de Dargenon."

So that was the true story. Half of Alani's blood and half of another's. Naomi couldn't be the dragon heir, because the heir had to be a Changeling. And if not Naomi, then who?

After spending hours researching in the library, Ez knew he couldn't put off delivering Naomi's letter for a moment longer. He soon arrived at the hotel where they were staying. He used the tracker to find her room and quickly slid the letter through her window. The process was quick, clean, and uncomplicated, unlike their relationship.

His mind knew that she could never forgive him, but his heart was too stubborn. Because there was no one in the world quite like Naomi. No one as strong, or as compassionate, or as fearless in every way a person could be. And he would do anything for her, dragon heir or not.

Anything.

Chapter 18: Paradise - (Ariah)

Somewhere in Time and Space

Ariah slipped off the number eight, but it was no mistake. It wasn't even a rash decision.

No, it was a perfect way out.

If she were to contemplate actual death, she'd have to account for the mystery of where she was going. Here, Ariah knew exactly where that was. She was off to a better place.

A place where she had never killed, lied, or betrayed.

A place where there was no war, and there would never be.

A place where Ez would always love her.

Paradise.

It's selfish, she thought. But how could it be? No one in the real world would miss her, not after she had betrayed them all.

As she fell, Ariah couldn't help but think of the irony of her entire situation. It was as if someone flipped karma right at the end of the storybook.

It truly was a villain's fairytale ending. She would get to live in a world where she wasn't the villain, while all of the heroes would suffer in the real world.

Chapter 19: Impromptu Messages - (Amethyst)

(Capital) Mae Lì: Northern Province, Tashiki

Amethyst enjoyed the fresh morning air of Mae Li, breathing in the clean snow and scented chimney smoke coming from the grand houses. She and the whole crew had left their cramped room in the hotel early in the morning, at varying levels of enthusiasm. Miko was leaping off the snow-covered roofs, nearly slipping several times on the polished round tiles. Grek was still hungover, and his sister didn't seem to have much patience for his groaning.

Naomi, reserved as ever, fussed with some letter that had appeared in their room yesterday.

Amethyst was beginning to get hungry, so she scouted the streets for an easy pickpocket. A few moments later, she settled on a woman with long, flowy pants. They must have been made of a soft fabric, because Amethyst could see the wallet-shaped bulge in the woman's pocket. So, Amethyst took the hair tie out of her bun and used it to attach her switchblade to her wrist. Then, she changed her walking course, so she could just barely skim the woman. That was enough time for Amethyst to stick out her palm and tear the fabric, allowing her to snatch the wallet without a glance.

Once she got back to her friends and the woman was out of sight, Amethyst opened the wallet. She counted the money and—Whoa! Five hundred dellum! Who keeps that kind of money in their pocket? Anyway, she was ecstatic, because it was probably the most money she'd ever had.

"Guys!" she said. "Who wants breakfast?"

After a quick stop at a nearby cafe, they sat down on a wooden bench and enjoyed what seemed like a feast. The sweet crumble of blueberry muffins, the salty ham of something called a quiche, and her personal favorite: a delectable pastry from the Northern Province called snowtart. They even got a copy of the newspaper, but Naomi told her to not spend any more money until they arrived at the palace.

And Amethyst was shocked at the front page of that newspaper.

Four People Killed in a Time Gap on Li Street

No, it couldn't be Li Street because that was... That was the very same street where Grek had passed out. Quickly, she crumpled up the paper and shoved it in her pocket. There was no point in obsessing over something that she barely understood. Taking a breath, she continued eating until everyone was ready to go.

"Gosh, I've missed coffee," Naomi sighed, relishing her last sip. "Alright, here's the plan..."

Miko hopped on her shoulder and everyone else circled around Naomi as she began to whisper. Really, they shouldn't be doing this out in the open, but what was the other option? "Grek, I want you to teach Heather how to pickpocket, as it's beginning to seem like the only useful skill we have now." Then she whispered something in the little snow monkey's ear, and he nodded. "Amethyst, you're with me. I want all of us to meet at the palace stables at 8 p.m. Understood?"

Everyone nodded. Naomi had just naturally been the leader, and though it wasn't something they had all decided on, everyone just accepted it. Something about her presence: the way she carried herself, the way she spoke... it was reminiscent of, well, a queen. But as everyone left and Naomi finally pulled out that letter, Amethyst saw that queen fall into tears.

How could one letter make someone as unbreakable as Naomi start sobbing like that? It was no secret that the princess had been through hell and back, but that piece of paper caused all the walls she had built to shatter.

"Are you okay?"

Naomi swiftly brushed the tears off her cheeks. "Yes, I'm fine. Sorry for my outburst. That letter just took me back two years." She started to stand but Amethyst grabbed her hand.

"You can trust me."

"That's just the thing, though. I can't trust anyone, because people take advantage of you. They hurt you and they use you and they break you, until there's nothing left but the pieces that you have to put back together. Because *everyone* is depending on me, and yet they don't care about me at all."

"Oh, Naomi..."

"All my life I thought people didn't worry about me, because they thought life as a princess was perfect. Of course, they were wrong, but at least they had an excuse. But now I'm not a princess,

I'm a witch, and those stupid shadows will never let me forget it. When I was fifteen, I learned my mom was a murderer, my best friend was a traitor, and my dad was a liar."

"I can't imagine what that was like. I never had anyone there, so no one could betray me. I don't know what I'd do if Grek did."

Now they were both sitting down on a stone bench, and Amethyst could feel Naomi's heart beating. It was just now that she realized just how much admiration she had for her. And after weeks of traveling together, they were finally becoming friends.

"Thank you," Naomi said. "For everything."

And then Naomi rested her head on Amethyst's shoulder, and though they were so different, it didn't matter anymore.

Chapter 20: The Girl from the Market - (Urumi)

(Capital) Mae Lì: Northern Province, Tashiki

Urumi wanted to scream. Urumi wanted to scream because he was in a room full of imbeciles. There were people dying, yes, dying! Nevertheless, the biggest concern of his planners was whether or not the unimportant silk of the unimportant tablecloths should be unimportantly imported from the finest silk factories. How was this palace not broke?

"Pardon me, Your Excellency," one of the planners called out. "Would you like to see a medic?"

What?

Urumi caught himself in a rather unnerved position. His fists were clenched and his knees were shaking. Quickly correcting this, he responded, "No. I would like to see an end to this meeting." The planner bit her lip, but Urumi only sighed.

"Advisor Lai specified that we were not to be dismissed early again. My apologies, my prince."

Urumi held back a snort. "I believe that prince overrules advisor, but I will wait it out if Lai so pleases." The woman looked utterly perplexed. He was starting to hate being a prince more and more. It was a sticky situation, of course, because he was given everything he wanted, but never taken seriously.

"So," another man began, "shall we get back to the task at hand, my prince?"

He groaned. "Of course." What were they talking about again? Brindimic cloths or Tashikian cloths? Oh right. This was ridiculous. "Just a simple blue cloth. After my meeting with the town hall representative, I will pick it up at the market."

"Cloth?" an old man replied. "But that's much too misfortunate. Two-hundred-and-forty-four years ago, a cloth was used, and the king spilled wine on his suit! No, we can't have a catastrophe like that happen again! For instance..." Urumi found himself drifting away, hearing only a few words here and there, paying attention to none of them. "And that is why kings and queens henceforth have come to disregard the possibility of cloths completely, and with rightful reason."

Urumi stopped slumping in his chair.

"I do not care if it was wine or his own blood on King Arkii III's suit that day, but the logically correct thing to do is to redirect at least some of the five-million dellum budget to better causes!"

The room fell silent. Once he spoke of time gaps, there was no going back. It was the ultimate wildcard in his limited deck.

"Local cloth it is," someone said as they jotted on a piece of parchment. Then, began the samples.

Five hours, forty-six minutes, and thirty-two seconds later, Urumi stood in a private hallway, staring at a portrait of his mother. She was young when she died; couldn't have been older than thirty. Her curly red locks stretched down to her waist, making her blue eyes shimmer. What had she been thinking at that moment? Was she afraid? Was she content? It was strange to see her looking almost as young as he. What a shock it would be when he woke up to find that he'd outgrown his own mother.

Urumi hadn't inherited her scarlet hair, though. Instead, he was a copy of his father's blond locks and tall build. It made him terrified of any mirror, looking up to see his father in his own reflection. Maybe it was because they were similar in so many ways. They had the same smile, his mother used to say. They had the same walk, the same hair, the same face. But most of all, they had the same unrelenting love for his mother. The only difference? Urumi had had the courage to let her die.

Well, maybe not. DRD was a failing response system, or more accurately, a normal one.

The formal definition was:

The Distorted Reality Disorder is a common effect on brains that have been psychologically pressured due to a specific past event. This may be anything from a traumatizing death to a stressful event. When the magic-based neurons in the brain interact with the logical, time-based receptors that receive and filter senses, especially that of sight, it causes the brain to have a confused, twisted perception of reality. This may result in severe hallucinations, unprovoked emotional outbreaks, a blurred vision, and/or suicidal conceptions.

He almost laughed at "suicidal conceptions." His father had died of a supposedly "accidental" overdose, but most people in the palace could fill in the blanks. Therefore, Urumi's definition of DRD was:

This is the disorder that ruined my father's life and is ready to do the same with mine.

That was definitely why he was so afraid of mirrors.

Urumi was woken by sirens. Everywhere. Guards rushed him out of his bed as his eardrums slowly died. Somewhere in the blurry distance he could hear someone yelling: "Evacuate the premises! Evacuate the premises!"

"Wait what…"

"My prince, we must leave immediately," a voice responded.

"It's the middle of the night. Surely it's just a mistake," he replied. He didn't move, refusing to lift his feet from the wooden floor. Why was he being so uncompliant? That he had no clue of. Ah, well. Lack of sleep and grogginess mixed together to form something Urumi called "horrible decisions."

"My prince," a guard said. "If you do not comply, we will evacuate you by force." He didn't budge. A few seconds later, his vision unblurred, and he realized that all the guards were at least a foot taller than him, and he was already being carried out of his room. For all the power a prince could have, he had none over his own fate.

They passed through at least ten full hallways before the sirens stopped beeping.

"Threat has been apprehended! Everyone please report back to their quarters!" a voice shouted. Just then, Lai came rushing through the door, a blue plume in hand.

"Prince Urumi, you must see this."

He blinked. "I'm confused."

"We believed that it was a group of bandits who wanted to steal from the treasury, but they are a very unusual cast, and they came unarmed."

"Lai, what are you speaking of?"

"Are you so misinformed?"

Urumi just nodded.

Lai continued, "I will show you."

"I would prefer this activity be performed while wearing a shirt, Advisor."

"Of course," Lai replied, and then stopped the next maid who ran by. "May you bring the prince a shirt, please?"

"Of course, Advisor Lai."

"Quickly, please," Lai urged. The maid scurried off.

A few minutes later, he and Lai sat in what appeared to be a poorly lit dungeon. After a few seconds of wasted silence, Lai finally decided to explain to him what this all was.

"A few people tried to break into the palace."

"At one in the morning?" Urumi groaned, fully aware of the dark bags under his eyes.

Preferably, this was not how one would present himself, but of course, preference didn't seem to take any part in being ruler.

"Yes," Lai said. "The attack was rather... questionable."

"Questionable how?" Before Lai could explain, a few guards dragged three people into the cell, with bars separating them from Urumi. Lai was right about one thing: the chained prisoners were rather strange. The first was a redheaded teenage girl, whom the guards brought into the light. She had flaming curls, and a stare that said: "I dare you to talk to me; we'll see what happens". Lai read out the information on her.

"Heather Queen. Six years old. Nationality: Valaztenian. Record: Dead."

Urumi blinked. What? "On to the next one, shall we?" The guards brought in a man, about sixteen or so, with dashing caramel hair, hazel eyes, and a daredevil smirk. He, Urumi had no trouble believing, was a criminal. "Grek Queen. Sixteen years old. Nationality: Tashikian. Former Nationality: Valaztenian. Record: Alive."

The next face needed no information spill. Her emerald green eyes were iconic. Her light brown skin was historic. How could someone not know that face? How could someone not know that indisputably, very, *very* dead girl? Yet here she was, indisputably alive.

"Princess Naomi Elistaire. Fifteen years old. Nationality: Valaztenian. Record: Dead."

"Oh, of what use to us is that record?" Urumi burst out. "It's fake!" He cupped his face in his hands. "Are there any more?"

"Yes," a guard replied. "A snow monkey that came with their forces is in special containment, and the last assailant has just finished her interrogation." Urumi lifted his head from his hands.

"I do not think that is an appropriate use of the word assailant, and I would prefer if it is not used again."

"Of course, my prince," the guard replied.

"Here is the captive." Urumi gasped. It was impossible to not recognize her. That hair that he had seen at the market... Why was she here? Was it horrible of him to be happy about her presence? Wait, how could she be in a jail cell? Was it even worse of him to be more jealous toward the man she came with than worried about the disaster of this all? Yes, he concluded. Yes, it was.

He wanted to hide. He wanted to go before she found out he was a prince—no. No use anymore, because she was already looking straight at him, her jaw almost as wide open as his.

"Are you going to read the information?" he asked Lai.

"My prince, there is none."

Chapter 21: The Dead Rebel Princess - (Naomi)

(Capital)Mae Lì: Northern Province, Tashiki

Naomi sneered. Between being chased through the capital city by guards, hiding in a barn stall, getting discovered by a large-mouthed scullery maid, being interrogated, earning the title of assailant, and being dragged through a dungeon in chains, she wasn't sure what was the best part of her *spectacular* day. To top it all off, Amethyst kept acting like an idiot, fumbling around like some kind of lunatic. Dear gosh, she was starting to sound like her mother.

She could hear some guards muttering about the mammalian savage in the other room. Or, as normal people called him, Miko.

"This is ridiculous!" Heather said, cursing. "I've been stuck in a freakin' cage for the better part of my life, and just 'cause some spoiled prince says so, here I am again!"

"He's not spoiled," Amethyst said from across the room, trying to claw off the chains on her feet. Heather and Grek laughed. Naomi didn't care enough.

"At least you don't have anything on your papers!" Heather said. "According to my files, I'm six. And dead!" Naomi fake coughed, and Heather turned around. "Oh right. You too."

"I'm gonna die listening to you all complain," a guard said. Heather smiled.

"When? Give me the date; I bet it'll be quite a show."

He yanked her hair. She grabbed his keys.

"Girl! Under demand of the royal guard, you must legally return those keys." Heather faked a thinking face, which looked kind of like the bobblehead pictures she'd draw of people when bored.

"Let me think..." she said. "No."

The whole scene reminded Naomi of the first time she had met Ez. The guard grabbed a spare key, opened the door, and Heather began to fight him for the keys. Of course she could beat him easily, but Heather taunted him, like dangling a piece of food in front of a hamster to make it run. Quickly, it got tiring for the spectators. Naomi had had enough of this nonsense.

"My name is Naomi Elistaire. I am seventeen, and if I wasn't marked as dead, I would be the Queen of Valaztein. Who is a lowly guard to refuse a queen-in-waiting a meeting with the prince?" The guard stood still.

"Bring him here," Amethyst said. "Then see what he'll do."

Surely enough, two hours later, despite the guard's hesitance, the prince had managed to return to see them after he cleared his "oh so busy" schedule. Turns out some things are more important than the fate of the world. Finally, Prince Urumi entered the room. Even if she was supposed to bow, the chains on her feet eliminated that possibility.

"Princess Naomi," the prince said. "I was told you seek to speak with me."

"You were told correctly," she replied. The prince's eyes kept twitching towards Amethyst; it was strange.

"What would you like to say?" he asked.

"First, I realize that this is a fairly horrible greeting for a prince, but that is hardly my fault. I apologize, partially. Second, I hope you recognize my predicament, as well as yours, considering the fact that with the flick of a hand, I could break your feeble chains. I'd also like to warn you that after two years in handcrafted hell, I might be just a tad bit insane. Third, this is a most horrible way for a person, never mind a king-in-waiting, to treat fellow refugees running from a murderous tyrant. Fourth, I'm afraid your country has played and will play an important role in the Valazteinian Civil War, seeing as if you help me, Miranda will kill you, and if you don't, someone else will. If you do help me, however, and protect the thousands of Valazteinian refugees, who I suspect have already arrived here, it would be greatly appreciated. Where should we start then? Oh yes, what about removing these bindings?"

The prince blinked. Silence clung to the moment for a few seconds.

"Of course," he replied. "Remove these bindings at once." The guards were quick to work, and soon Naomi, Heather, Amethyst, and Grek were all out of their bindings and on a comfortable palace sofa outside the dungeons.

"Now," Naomi said, partly to the guards, partly to Prince Urumi, "could you please release Miko from his wretched incarceration."

"Who?" a guard asked.

"Oh right. The mammalian savage." She had to stop being so sarcastically unapproachable. She couldn't really stop herself, though. And it was clearly doing the trick, because Miko was back in her arms in a matter of seconds.

"I will arrange for a meeting with my cabinet of advisors in three hours. Forgive me for the rough welcome," Prince Urumi said.

"Wasn't much of a welcome," Heather grumbled.

"Thank you," Naomi said. "My apologies for the impromptu appearance."

Prince Urumi nodded and began walking towards the door.

"The maids will lead you to your quarters." He shut the door. Wow, Naomi was surprised that she still remembered her princess talk. It had been quite a long time since it had been necessary.

A few minutes later, a maid came and called Naomi to the meeting. She had passed countless hallways and staircases before they finally came upon a large room with a gigantic marble table. She was the last to enter. To her left sat Heather, Grek, Amethyst, and Miko (who somehow had a seat of his own), and on her right, at the head of the table, sat Prince Urumi. In front of her were ten of the king's advisors, nine for specific subjects and one overall. Again, Prince Urumi seemed to throw a glance Amethyst's way every few seconds, and the same said of her. Finally, he called the meeting to order.

"Princess Naomi," he began. "Do you have anything to say?"

This was it. The make-or-break moment. If she messed up now, there was nothing more she could say to fix it.

"Yes. A few weeks ago, I launched an escape with thousands of my people from the Elemento Tribe Territories in Valaztein. Unfortunately, we were detected by one of the Queen's military ships. Heather, Miko, and I went up to the ship and disabled its radiation system. After we accomplished this, we were spotted by guards and knocked into the ocean. While my people continued to the capital, Heather, Miko, and I arrived in Kry, where Amethyst and Grek saved us. From there, we decided to travel to the capital to seek you. The Queen's guards were constantly in pursuit of us, so we had to hide in rather unconventional places to escape. I ask of you temporary shelter, and a refuge for my people. As well as this, I was wondering if you would be willing to lend a hand in the movement against Queen Miranda. She has massacred our people, destroyed our land, ruined what we believe in, and extinguished every flame of hope for a better future. Please, help us."

The prince discussed this with his advisors for about a half hour, though there wasn't really much to discuss. The prince either had a conscience, or he didn't. As simple as that. Finally, someone came to a conclusion. At least she thought they did, because the room fell quiet. All eyes were on the prince, including hers.

"After careful consideration, my advisors and I have come to a decision. We will provide shelter to Princess Naomi and her Valezteininan refugees, and the possibility of battlefield aid will be discussed after my coronation." Naomi nearly leaped out of her chair in joy. She had done it! And then he kept talking. "If their stay in the palace causes any kind of trouble or harm to my citizens, they will be imprisoned and sent to Queen Miranda immediately." Oh crap.

A few nights later, Naomi had acquired a new habit. Pacing through the palace dungeons, trying to control her ever-growing powers. After not using them for quite a while, her shadows were shrieking in her mind. Kind of like a bored body bursting for exercise. The only difference was that exercise was normal; her powers weren't.

She was in a dark cell in the deepest part of the dungeons—pretty much a man-made cavern. When she sat down, Naomi saw a piece of paper right beside her. A letter. Out of pure curiosity, she checked who it was addressed to.

Oh, gosh... How? Why? It was addressed to her father, which meant that he must have been a prisoner, wouldn't it? She opened the letter; even her terror couldn't stop her impulse.

Dear Nicholae,

I hope you rot in hell. If you believe for one second that I don't know who you are or where you're hiding it, then you are sadly mistaken. I will find that creature before Jiko has the time to say sorry. Don't you understand? I know Anaji's harboring fugitives; people that should be dead! And right after I kill you, slowly and painfully, I will kill her, too. Or perhaps I'll kill her first, so that you can have the pleasure of watching.

Why do you have to make everything so complicated, Nikki? We have two beautiful daughters and a whole kingdom. Don't you love them more than your dragon fantasies?

Never mind, it's too late.

And in case you're wondering, yes, the shadows have come for me. I doubt you care, but I wanted you to know this before you die, Nikki. Just because I'm going to kill you doesn't mean I don't love you. In fact, they're quite often the same thing.

Sincerely,
Miri

Chapter 22: Checkmate - (Ez)

```
(Capital)Mae Lì: Northern Province, Tashiki
```

Ez sat on a log, trying to cook some venison in the churning fire on the outskirts of the capital city, while Zyon was out scouting in the city. Every time Ez's cooking failed, he'd spit out an impressively long line of curse words, none of which ten-year-old Daunt should be hearing. After a few more failed attempts, he finally gave up, kicking the ground before falling silent. Ez was perfectly happy with retreating into his thoughts. Of course, he forgot who was next to him.

Daunt began fidgeting. But it was no small fidget. It started with his hands playing around with a stick, to his feet starting to thump on the ground, and his legs shaking for no reason at all. Then he began humming an upbeat tune. Long story short, the boy was a sound machine and Ez didn't plan on dancing along with the beat.

"La, la, la, la, la la, la, la, la, la, la."

"Daunt, can you be quiet for one second?" The irritation in his voice was obvious. Daunt nodded.

"Okay." Maybe the hyperactive boy was trying his best at silence, but all Ez knew was that out-of-tune humming did not make it easy to think. On anything.

"Daunt," he said again, losing patience. "Please."

Daunt obeyed… mostly. Ez did his best to ignore it.

Instead, he continued to think about the recent events. Some people would tell him to cry; let his emotions out to roam freely, but he didn't want to cry. He wanted to scream, he wanted to yell, he wanted to throw daggers at the ground, but he didn't want—he couldn't bring himself to cry. Maybe, most likely, he just didn't care enough to. Why did it even matter if she was dead or alive? A traitor was a traitor. No matter—

"La, la, la, la, la la, la, la, la, la, la—" Oh not again.

"Daunt, shut up!" Daunt stilled. He took in the quiet, no, the *silence*. And he looked afraid. He looked terrified. What had Ez done? "Daunt, I'm sorry." The boy turned his head up slowly. Daunt looked like he was going to burst out screaming, but he didn't.

"I went to that noisy forest for a reason, you know." Daunt paused.

"You can trust me, Daunt."

"My dad wasn't such a great person. He hit my mom, and my sister too, and sometimes me." Ez winced. Naomi's past flashed through his head. "So, one day…" Daunt was breaking up. "My sister told me that she was gonna run away. From our home. Far away from the Western Province. She wanted me to come with her. I wanted to too, so I did. We were going to the Northern Province, but…"

"Hey, you don't have to tell me this."

"No, I want to. Because I don't want you to ever complain about how much I talk, or how I can never stay still. The entrance fee to the Northern Province isn't just for the Southern Province. It's for where I come from too. They don't let people from the Western Province in without their money. When we reached the border, we had no idea of the rules. After seeing the poster, my sister and I hid in a bush." He wiped a tear. "She told me to stay there while she figured this out. So I did. I stayed hidden. I stayed safe. It was the worst thirty seconds of my life. She screamed and yelled at the officer standing on the border. Her pain was so loud, until it wasn't. She ran right towards the fence, but the officer shot her down before she could even touch it. And then she was quiet forever, and it was that silence, that emptiness... not even the rage she had felt only a few seconds before was worse. I ran away. That's why I called myself Daunt. Because if I had been braver, I could've saved her."

"Daunt..." Ez pulled him in tight. How was this possible? Daunt of all people? So bubbly and childish?

"I'll never go quiet," Daunt said.

And then shadows shot from the sky.

In an instant, Daunt was no longer in his grasp. He was in the fierce grip of shadows, or more accurately, his throat was. Everything was drowned out by Daunt's screams.

Miranda. Of course, not in person.

"Hello, Ez," she cackled.

"I'd say it's nice to see you. But..."

"Oh," she said. "Don't worry about offending me. It's not." The grip on Daunt got tighter.

"Help! Help!"

"What do you want, Miranda?"

"Oh, I'm sure you'll find my offer very... benevolent."

After a two-minute conversation with Miranda, Ez was trapped. Every way out was a dead end in this insane deal she had proposed. How much was he willing to give up? Was this really a solution?

"Miranda, I'd never..."

"Or would you?" She smirked, tightening the shadows' grip on Daunt. "Checkmate." The shadows disappeared, once more blending into the ever-growing darkness. Daunt collapsed to the ground, tearful, but breathing. Ez wasted no time collecting their provisions. He grabbed Daunt and started running. Running towards the nearest light he could see. Because his encounter with Miranda could mean two things. That her powers had grown beyond imaginable, giving her the ability to use them across entire oceans, or she was already here, in the capital of Tashiki. Either way, Naomi was doomed. They all were.

Chapter 23: Mr. Prince - (Amethyst)

(Capital)Mae Lì: Northern Province, Tashiki

Amethyst tried not to fall asleep in another meeting that, for some reason, she *had* to take part in. Why? Well, maybe they hadn't realized just how little she understood them. Even in her nice new clothes, she felt so out of place in the finely decorated meeting hall. Despite being in the prince's closest companionship, nothing changed from who she was back in Kry: a penniless thief.

And she wasn't sure if seeing Urumi was an upside or a downside to all this madness. On the good side, she got to see him. On the bad side, he was going to become her most despised profession and all of Tashiki's most despised profession... just saying. After being abused and mistreated by the government, Amethyst couldn't help but roll her eyes at him. Why would a spoiled prince be any better than his negligent dad?

Eventually, her anger topped it all, as it usually did, and she proceeded to mock his royal majesty. After that uninspiring conference, Lodem—no Urumi, held her a little after. Of course, half of his royal guard was watching. Urumi glanced at her with an odd sincerity.

"I hope you're finding your stay here pleasant."

She was supposed to bow to *his royal highness* now, right? *Pft*, what a joke, which is exactly what she took her bow as. Yes, it was a mocking, over-exaggerated curtsy.

"Oh yes. Very pleasant indeed. My prince." She let the last few words linger. This was ridiculous; now she was just being cruel. He had been so generous to welcome them into the palace. But on the other hand... lying had been cruel, too. Besides, he could stand for someone to tell him off once in a while! Obviously, no one in this stuffy mansion did. Unfortunately, Urumi didn't look flustered by how she had reacted. Instead, he ambled towards his guards.

"I will be at the palace gardens at five-thirty today if the lady cares to join me. Put that on that schedule." His advisors were quick to argue.

"But, my prince—"

"Surely we can clear off thirty minutes?" As the agitated advisors fumbled over schedules, Amethyst caught Urumi sneaking a grin. "Wonderful." And then he strolled out the door, enveloped in his cocoon of guards. A cocky wink accompanied his princely stride.

She was going to kill him.

○

Despite herself, Amethyst walked into the palace gardens at five-thirty on the dot. Below a striking blossom tree, Urumi sat on a marble bench, a scarlet rose in hand. His laced-up boots were covered by pearly white snow, and his golden-blond curls shimmered in the afternoon sun. He jumped up when he saw her and grinned. Amethyst's heart raced as he wrapped his jacket around her and handed her the rose.

"How cliché," was all she said. Yet despite herself, she reached for the bright flower.

"Would it ease your discomfort to know that I questioned it several times with my advisors?"

"No, it would not."

Whoa, the frigid temperature hit like a chilly blast in her lavender cotton dress. The Southern Province was like an eternal desert; she'd never even seen snow before coming here. This moment, the way the sunlight was glimmering off of the powdery snow and onto Urumi's smile... maybe she did like the winter.

A maid passed through, probably trying to catch a glimpse of the kind of girl the prince had brought to a romantic outing. Amethyst swiftly sat down and turned away. They certainly wouldn't be expecting someone like her. "And can you please talk like a normal person?"

"Look, my apologies—"

"Ahem," she interrupted.

He blinked. "I'm sorry for being so deceitful in my manner of—"

"Ahem!"

He was quicker to catch on this time, shortening the phrase.

"I'm sorry for lying."

"Much better." Amethyst sighed. Here she sat, in a beautiful garden by a handsome prince, and she was still holding on to all her anger! Well, how could she not? Urumi had no idea what she had gone through because of his family and yet—the world calmed down when she was around him. So, she was ready to put some things behind her. "And as much as I hate myself for this, I forgive you. Kind of. Ish."

"Is that the best I'm going to get?"

"Yep."

"Ah well. Good enough." There were now four maids giggling from behind a bush, watching the scene play out.

"Any place more private where we can talk?"

She glared at the maids, who quickly scurried off to a different bush.

"Of course." He grabbed her hand and showed her through expansive fields of lilies and jadenips, dazzling rows of white roses, and even ponds of frozen tulips. How could so much beauty grow in the snow? Finally, they arrived at a clearing of lavish green foliage. Strangely, it seemed less tamed than the rest of the other trimmed and polished gardens. She just kept following the stone path, but he turned her around so she faced a wall covered in leaves.

Apparently, it wasn't just a wall, because he swung a piece of it open. It led to a spectacular scene of red cherry blossoms and two oak swings that served as seats.

"You had this planned all along didn't you, Mr. Prince?" The nickname might have been a little mocking, but mostly endearing. Honestly, she was disappointed at how quickly she had let her anger crumble away. Oh well, there wasn't much she could do now; the guy had charm.

"Mr. Prince?" he asked.

"You don't want me to call you that?"

"You ask it as if I had a say in the matter."

She smiled. "Fair point."

Urumi chuckled, his entire face lighting up with a warm smile. Amethyst looked up, gazing at the beautiful sun setting on the faraway horizon. Rays of golden light shone through the branches of the cherry blossom trees.

"Shall I bring us some firelight?" he asked.

"Why not?" He grabbed a nearby candle and took a box of matches from his pocket.

After about forty seconds of failed candle-lighting, she asked, "What's the holdup?"

"Just one moment." Amethyst turned around to see him vigorously trying to light the match. She held in a laugh, but he could sense it. "I suppose I've just always had someone to, I guess I just never, I know if I—"

"You can't light a candle?" she teased.

"It's harder than it seems!" Amethyst just laughed some more.

"Sorry," she said between giggles. Finally, her body allowed her to stop. Swinging the match, she brought a nice, healthy flame to the candle. Urumi feigned sadness.

"Ah well, I guess I'll just have to ask you to dance to make up for it." She bit her lip.

"Oh, no."

"Oh, yes." He held his hand out, and Amethyst realized that she'd make him look like a fool if she didn't take it. And maybe, just maybe, despite her lousy dancing skills, she wanted to.

"There's not even music!"

"Who says there needs to be music?"

"Okay," she said. "I'm gonna stop you right there. Way too cheesy."

"Got it." He grinned, then gasped. "Wait... you don't know how to dance, do you?"

She stayed silent, embarrassed. "Yeah."

"'Yeah?' This is worse than my matches incident!"

"Is not!" she argued.

"Is so!" They continued arguing like this a few more times, until neither of them could continue and both burst out laughing.

"So," Amethyst said. "Tell me one truly spectacular thing about you, Mr. Prince."

"Besides the fact that I got you to hold my hand? Maybe that I've never failed a test." Amethyst burst out giggling. She laughed and laughed and laughed some more. Urumi looked annoyed. "Why are you laughing?" She slowed herself down and was finally able to commit to a verbal response.

"You don't have many friends, do you, Mr. Prince?"

"Hey!" He sighed. "Okay, that might be true." She wasn't really paying attention, though; Amethyst was too busy admiring his bright cerulean eyes.

"I take that back," she said. "You're too cute to have no friends." He grinned a lovely, wide-eyed grin.

"Tell me one truly spectacular thing about *you,* Lady Amethyst."

"Is that an order?"

"No, it's a request."

"Good, 'cause I think you know by now that I don't take orders from anybody. Especially a prince." Perhaps that was the most hilarious thing anyone had said all evening. Because here she was, with a man she had concluded to despise, in a place she hated of mere envy, swaying to music she didn't want to hear. And yet... it was there. A gentle tune whistled in her heart, impossible to miss.

Chapter 24: The Drift - (Naomi)

(Capital) Mae Li, Tashiki

Naomi's head spiraled as she sprung out of her linen and gold bed sheets. Despite the luxurious comfort, her eyes had barely closed all night. The coronation was fast approaching, and that meant Urumi would soon change the world's history forever. As a king, he would have full military power, which meant he could side with Miranda or Naomi in the upcoming war.

Therefore, worry took priority over sleep. And to be completely honest, all she did was worry.

Worry about Miranda's hellish plans to destroy the world.

Worry about all the lies her father was too dead to explain.

Worry about Heather's precarious past.

Worry about Amethyst's involvement with the prince.

Worry about Ez's letter.

Oh no, why was she so caught up in all of this? For now, she had to focus on the simple tasks ahead of her: a comb and a dress. So she brushed her raven-colored locks, relishing the familiar knots and tangles. The delicate bristles not only calmed her hair but also her nerves. Really, she was quite overdue for a haircut, but her now hip-length hair, though unpractical, reminded her of Naira's.

She splashed some cool water on her face from the marbled sink basin and then inspected her clothing prospects for the day. The palace maids rotated and added new gowns to the closet every day, each more lovely than the last. Yes, it was unlike her to take so much pleasure in garments and grooming, but it was comforting to know it was a pleasure she could afford.

Today, she picked out a cotton blue dress with a silver hem and a lacey corset. Finally, she clipped a few jadenips to her hair and set off to the many meetings she needed to attend.

There's no need to worry, she promised herself. But how could she not? There were a million unanswered questions that could very well take a life. If she wasn't having delusions that day in the burning cabin and Ez had dropped off that letter by hand... Could it be that he was in Tashiki?

Now her prior promise certainly felt foolish, because there was *everything* to worry about in a coronation where shadows and Changelings would be in attendance.

The moonlight shimmered on the snowflakes that fell from Naomi's window. She lounged on a velvet cushion in her room, gazing out into the luminous night. The day had been tiring, so she was thankful for this moment of quiet solitude. That was until Heather ran in screaming.

"I am going to *kill* that spoiled brat and his two-faced army of idiots!"

Her dark curly hair was tied back in a messy braid, and she yanked at a rosy crimson dress that she clearly wasn't too comfortable in. All the rolling her eyes were doing only drew attention to the dark bags under them. "Elistaire, how did you survive half of your life in a palace with those pompous jerks?"

Well, it looked like Heather wasn't having the easiest time adjusting. Naomi tried to be supportive, but there was just too much whining going on currently for Heather to be anything but irritating.

"Not sure," she said, returning to her window.

Heather sat down next to her. "Oh, come on. Do they seriously not frustrate you?" Naomi turned around, meeting her gaze.

"Of course they do, but at some point, you have to accept who has the power."

"Pft," Heather replied. "Then they should find something better to do with it than judge people. They don't know anything about what I've gone through."

"Neither do I," Naomi sighed, finally letting it out. "And since you don't ever feel like telling me about your past, I think our conversation is finished."

Heather jerked back in her seat, glaring at Naomi with a furrowed brow. Gosh, now she'd really ticked a nerve. And yet... Heather didn't start to yell.

"You want to know about my past, huh?" she said. "You want to know about how your psycho mom abused children? Well, here you go: I was turning five the day I was taken."

"Taken? By who?"

"Guess." Her mother? What? Why? Despite Naomi's look of confusion, Heather continued. "I lived in Dopül, with my two older brothers, Alem and Grek, and my dad."

"But why would she take you?"

"We call it the Drift. Some years ago, the Queen started collecting kids for her 'programs.' That's why she took me. They teach us how to murder at specialized camps. We're the Queen's group of assassins."

"What about Alem, and how did Grek wind up in Tashiki?" Naomi asked as she inched closer to Heather.

"Grek had run away to Tashiki after a fight with Dad, and Alem... well, he was taken too." Heather paused and turned her head upward, refusing to bear a tear. "I don't know what happened to my dad. I assume he was killed, and Grek stayed in Tashiki."

"And Alem?"

"Do you know about the Queen's Black magic system? The real reason everything's running in Valaztein?" Naomi nodded. The shock when she figured out that Miranda used human energy to fuel Valaztein's magic was indescribable. But... whose energy was it? "Well, only a part of the kids the Queen recruits are of service to her, and those who are she calls strong. The weak... they're the energy source for the Queen's system of Black magic."

More people dying, because she had failed to stop the Queen; because she had failed her people.

"Are you wondering how I know?" Heather asked, a maddening laugh escaping her. Those brown eyes glared into Naomi's skull. "Alem was labeled weak. The next time I saw him, he was barely a carcass of a boy; like death, but worse." Heather pounded at the seat, once again holding back tears.

"Heather..."

"Don't pity me!" She was screaming now, but then her voice went down to a silent whisper. "'Cause you know what? The labels are all wrong. The weak are too strong to bend their conscience, and the strong are too weak to protect it. I went crazy, Elistaire. I still am."

Naomi wanted to hug her, to say that she was sorry for making her relive such terrible moments of her past. All she wanted to do was shield this little girl from these horrors, but Heather had already faced them.

"I needed to get out. I had to. So, I went rogue. After years in a camp, the best of the crop were transferred to an elite training center in the palace, and that included me. A friend of mine helped me hack into the palace messaging system, where instead of finding a plausible way of escape, I found your location in the Crown Maze. A few days later, I struck a deal with one of Miranda's associates: your whereabouts in exchange for a way out for me and my friend. The man said he was under too much surveillance, so I created a gap in the Maze for you to get out, per his request. So, he gave me the evidence and info I needed in case any kind of trial ever came up."

"What happened to your friend?" Naomi asked. Heather replied with an eerie fury.

"Stabbed to death with a knife."

"What was his name?" Naomi asked.

"Zyon." Heather then let a single tear streak down her face, and she didn't stop it. "This is why I don't want Grek to know. I don't want him to see the type of monster they made me into."

"I won't tell him, I promise."

Heather smiled.

"Thank you." She paused. "I don't think I can ever use a knife again. Not after what I did to you. Not before what I can still do to Grek."

"I don't see why you'd have to." Then Naomi remembered when she'd first met Heather. "Wait, did you think I was my mother?"

"Well, I don't know if anyone's ever told you this, Elistaire, but you two have a striking resemblance."

Naomi resisted the urge to jump with glee. Heather hadn't wanted to kill her. Even once. Then Naomi was brought back to reality by an overwhelming curiosity.

"Heather, I've got one more question for you. If you don't mind me asking, what was the name of the man you struck a deal with?"

Heather didn't flinch.

"The White Joker."

Chapter 25: Instructions From the Dead - (Urumi)

(Capital) Mae Lì: Northern Province, Tashiki

Urumi leaped out of bed like a hyperactive child. Of course, this was a very unkingly habit for an oh, so kingly occasion. It was today! The day his life would change forever; the day he could start changing others' lives forever. Coronation day. All the silks, linens, cloths, fancy ornaments, crazy speech writers, and buffets vs. set menu vs. ordering vs. blah, blah, blah… It was all over!

Yes, he would still have to attend to foolish palace mannerisms after the coronation, but for one day he could focus only on what was important: stopping the time gaps, regaining Tashiki's financial stability, and easing the tense relations with Valaztein. Goodness, his father certainly left him with many messes to clean up.

Still, not much changed from his usual morning schedule. It was planned by the second, every hour of every day. How else was he to avoid wasting valuable time? It went something like this—no, *exactly* like this:

First, he woke at three fifty-seven in the morning. (A nearly impossible task, considering he had stayed up signing documents until midnight. Fortunately, he was one of the very few people who could run on four hours of sleep.)

Next, showering, dressing, and grooming his blond curls took up exactly thirty-three minutes.

Then, his breakfast would be delivered to his quarters at four-thirty, quite perfect timing, and he would begin making himself aware of the ever-frustrating problem with the press. Those petty magazines wrote so scandalously that they could have the entire country believing anything. Maybe there was a reason why freedom of speech wasn't in the Valazteinian constitution. Oh wow, that was not very kingly of him.

After a twelve-minute breakfast and press annotation, he signed more documents. Despite all his staff's work, the prince would always end up on paper duty. That took exactly one hour and fifty-five minutes.

Later came the formal breakfast. Obviously, he couldn't actually *eat* in the formal breakfast. No, no, no. This was because he always had some lord or advisor or even ruler at the table as well. He had learned quite young that hunger led to bad decisions during meetings. Certainly, his opponent couldn't be handed the upper hand. *Opponent* might seem like a poor choice of words, but trust him, it wasn't.

That day, his breakfast had been with his stylist, who couldn't seem to choose between the silver, copper, or gold prototype for his suit's pin. As easily imaginable, it was not a pleasant breakfast. Ah well, dull and stuffy were better than royally deranged. Afterward, Lai met him at the threshold of a long marble stairwell.

"Prepared, king-in-waiting?" Lai said.

"Please, call me Urumi. I need one thing to be somewhat regular today."

"You feign nervousness, but clearly represent excitement."

Urumi sighed. It was easy to forget how precisely Lai read his mind. "Correct, as always."

"I suspect your anxiety towards one procedure, though." Urumi bit his lip, not looking forward to the following lecture.

"Must you always read my mind?"

"It is an important part of the coronation ceremony, and you shall not break an ancient tradition due to fear of your ancestry," Lai said as he strode down the stairs.

"What if I see him, Lai?"

"The selection is from all the past rulers of Tashiki. Do you truly believe that your father will be the one chosen?"

"Why take the risk? The Line Between the Living and the Dead is an old tradition. We could tell the people that we are forsaking it in terms of modernization."

"You are intelligent in many things, but this is clearly not one of them."

Urumi wanted to interrupt, but let his advisor continue. "Don't you understand? The argument you just made is exactly why we must continue The Line Between the Living and the Dead. It is an ancient procedure; people receive comfort knowing that their past rulers will be able to communicate with their upcoming one, even if only for five minutes. Besides, what exactly do you believe the frivolous press will assume if you bypass this particular tradition?"

Urumi stayed quiet for a moment.

"Mentally unfit, daddy issues... I know the deal."

"Correct."

Urumi just nodded, because deep down, he knew Lai was right.

Terror dominated before he walked into the open coronation hall. Anxiety attacked his body, causing sweat to creep down the back of his tightly fitted white and gold suit. Urumi recalled the sound of his father's whiskey bottle shattering on the floor of that very same hall.

Ever since the death, he'd pushed away all those unpleasant memories of his weak-willed, grief-ridden father. What if that stupid tradition resurfaced them on the day he was supposed to be leaving his past behind?

"You're going into a palace hall, not a dragon's den," Lai said, ever supportive by his side.

"You're right. Dragons are extinct, along with my father, so I should have nothing to worry about," he replied.

"She would be proud of you."

With that, Urumi strode into that room, carrying his presence with a stubborn pride he never knew he had. With honor at who he had become. Just knowing, just feeling in his heart that his mother would be weeping on the stands at this moment, gave him strength. He strolled through that aisle, accepting of all the duty that befell upon him as a king. To be a king was to balance virtues for the greater good. To rule with pride, yet humility. To punish with strength, yet tolerance. He was a carrier of love and hatred; ideals he would nurture for the rest of his life. For his kingdom. For his people. For his mother. For Lai. For Amethyst. For Tashiki.

The master of ceremonies stood on a large obsidian pedestal, prepared for the upcoming events. Thankfully, unlike other Tashikian procedures, coronation ceremonies were straightforward and to the point.

"Recite the vows of the Line Between the Living and the Dead."

"I, Prince Urumi of Tashiki, vow to cross the line between life and death with the virtues and duties bestowed upon me in the commandments of our sacred oaths."

"Gontagar."

"Gontagar." A sorcerer's necklace made of dark gemstones was placed over his neck, but he would not let this disturb him. He had to remember that though no one in the audience could hear him or his dead ancestors, they could easily see his reactions. He had to stay calm. Just as expected, the world turned purple.

Urumi awoke to the sound of the ocean. The gentle waves crashed against nearby rocks, and he could feel the soft sand on his feet. This was the first thing that surprised him. Instead of his suffocating suit, Urumi was wearing a loose, cream-colored shawl and navy pants. A figure materialized, made completely of sand. In an instant, Urumi could tell who it was.

Just his luck. He stared up at the reincarnation of his father.

"What do you want?"

"Urumi, please. Forgive me for—"

The nerve! How could he dare ask for forgiveness? Clearly, his father was unhinged.

"Guess there's no alcohol in hell, huh?" *Keep it together. Keep it together.*

"There isn't much time. The ancestors did not even approve of this meeting originally."

"What is wrong with you?" There was nothing Urumi could do about rogue emotions now. Only to try not to cry. "Life gives you more time, and *this* is how you use it?"

"You don't understand."

"What don't I understand?" Unshed tears burned to be let free in his eyes. Urumi had to stop before it was too late. His father's sand figure started fading away in the wind, and over the violent gusts he could hear his father say, "Visit your mother's grave!"

When he returned, the master of ceremonies took back the gemstone necklace.

"Bow to me, and recite the vows." What he did next was quite spontaneous and even he did not expect it. Turning around, Urumi faced his people who stood diligently in the extensive pews of the palace hall. It was to them that he bowed.

The master of ceremonies sighed as Urumi recited the vows. "I now pronounce you King Urumi of Tashiki!" He wanted to cry, but not tears of anxiety, or anger, or grief. Joy overwhelmed him when he glanced at Amethyst and Lai applauded along with thousands of others in the crowd. Amethyst cheered wildly, while Lai showed a polite applaud, equally excited despite his meager expression.

Urumi was nearly too ecstatic to notice the roaring shadows looming over the mighty hall.

Chapter 26: Fire and Shadows - (Naomi)

(Capital) Mae Lì: Northern Province, Tashiki

Naomi ran like the world depended on it.

And honestly, it probably did.

There was nothing she could do to end the shadows, or the deaths of those who had been lost to them. All she could do now was keep running; running and trying to save those whom she could.

"Please!" cried a frail woman. "Take my child!" As Naomi grabbed the bawling toddler, the woman trembled away from the black monsters about to claim her life, muttering a prayer.

Oh, how Naomi wished there was some higher power up there.

But no god was coming to save her tonight.

"Your child will be alright," Naomi whispered.

The woman only nodded, sobbing. Naomi searched around for any means of escape. The shadows were blocking every gate and door. They murdered anyone who tried to leave.

But doors weren't the only way out of a palace... So, Naomi had around five people huddled in the air vents, which had been spotted as the only viable escape route. Quickly, she found Grek and

Heather. While the three tried to evacuate as many people as possible to the air vents, Grek's new friend/girlfriend/hookup, Analuna, led several escapes through the air vents. She had come up with an efficient system, and it seemed to be working perfectly. It was astounding how quickly she went from "pretty, but useless" to "smart and resourceful." Grek had looked even more surprised, seeing as their bond had been formed at the cocktail bar just thirty minutes before the coronation, but they continued evacuating people.

"Heather! Go help that man over there!" Grek shouted.

"Got it!"

Naomi currently carried a light old woman whom she had found weeping by the corpse of a man. Well, she wasn't sure if she could call it a corpse. It was more of an ashen shadow.

As much as she tried to avoid it, it was inevitable not to use her powers at least once or twice during her endeavor.

"HEATHER!" Grek screamed from in front of her. "BEHIND YOU!" Heather just managed to dodge the attacking shadow, but a shadow skimmed her shoulder, and she fell to the ground in pain. Her shoulder was scarlet and dripping with blood. They both rushed to her side.

"Can you walk?"

"Yeah, yeah. I'm fine."

"No, you're not!" Grek swept falling hair from his face, his eyes a reflection of worry and stress.

"Get to Analuna!" Naomi told her.

"No, I wanna help."

"The best way you can help is by not dying," Grek replied. Despite her current state, Heather managed to stick her tongue out at her brother.

"Naomi, please let me—"

"That's an order!" Naomi shouted. Grek was right; they couldn't risk her getting hurt. "From your queen."

"Fine." Heather picked herself up and started trotting towards the air vent. They soon lost sight of her, and Grek took no care to hide his flustered expression.

"She's gonna be fine."

"I know," he replied, but it sounded more like he was trying to convince himself. As Grek eased his worry, Naomi made the mistake of looking out into the destruction. Creatures of shadow moved through the night with an eerie silence. The palace was engulfed by darkness. And the hall, once decorated by candles and flowers, stood deprived of any light. Screams ricocheted against the white walls, drowning out all other sounds.

Then, a scorching flame blazed in the darkness, inciting a battle to claim the night.

A great roar shook the earth.

Grek's jaw dropped. Oh, of course the Tashiki boy had never seen a dragon in his life.

"But dragons are... They've been extinct for years... How?" Extinct, what? Well, just another thing to add to her *"What Has Happened in the Last Two Years"* list.

"I wish I knew." Naomi failed to hide her shock, because looming fifty feet above her was a certain Changeling flashing scarlet scales. More than anything, those crystal blue eyes gave it away.

Ez.

"But—" Grek argued.

"We gotta go. This is not good news." Naomi yanked him by the arm, and they sprinted through the shrieking throngs. Uh, why the heck was he here? Hadn't he ruined her life enough?

"I don't understand. The dragon was chasing off the shadows; why'd we run?" Naomi held in her frustration. She had to, because Grek didn't know. He didn't know and there was no way he could've because she hadn't told him.

She hadn't told anyone.

Because history had proved people didn't deserve her trust.

Stopping next to a large banquet table topped with cracked macarons she said, "Of course you don't understand! How could you understand?" He only looked more perplexed.

"What?"

"Grek, just stay out of it."

"Okay," he replied. Naomi pulled him under the table as a shadow shot near her neck.

"First, we need to find Heather and Analuna."

"And then we need to get the hell out of here," Grek replied. "There's nothing else we can do."

"There's one thing."

"You've already used your voodoo magic enough."

"Close your eyes."

He did, because no one who had seen her magic would want to see it for a second time.

If only *she* could close her eyes. Inhale, exhale. It was time. A shadow nearly skimmed her ankle. Everything set back into action again, and Grek opened his eyes.

"Why are they shooting at us?!" he yelled.

"What do you think?" she yelled back. There could not have been a worse time to be in a long, lily-green gown. At least Grek got to be in a slightly more comfortable suit.

"Duck!" he screamed. She did, but then that same shadow hit an unsuspecting man behind her.

There was the guilt.

Despite it, Naomi got up and kept running.

Something shot up from the ground. Shadows. Large, repulsive indigo shadows that grasped her ankles and glued them in place. Of course, Miranda had just been playing before. The shadows ascended. Up. Up. Up. From her ankles to her knees, from her knees to her thighs, from her thighs to her waist. Her mother was making it so slow for a reason. To let the despair sink in first.

The shadows reached her torso, but she would not let them reach her arms. No, that was her last resort. And one she would have to use, she determined. And soon.

The world was a ticking clock, and she was stuck in the middle, deciding which hands to move to keep it running. A shadow knife breezed right by Grek, nearly stabbing him.

That was the last tick. She called upon the pieces of her fractured conscience and prayed that they could forget where they came from, if only for just a moment. Her hand shot out in Grek's direction, and so did the shadows that came with it. Once they hit the attacking shadows, she could easily compare them. The abundance of similarities was appalling, and there was only one small difference: the string of gold that passed through Naomi's shadows.

But what did that mean now? The crown Infitri's magic had placed upon her head had long been washed away, along with everything else that reminded her of that great loss. Of all the people that had betrayed her.

The shadows were real.

The shadows were now.

The shadows were terrifying.

All they did was link Naomi to her mother. Was her father able to see it in her eyes? Could he tell, even when she was little, what she was?

She was a sorceress.

She was a monster.

She was another reason why her father left.

How could this be happening? Why was she being forced to do this miserable thing?

Again? At least it was not on people. At least the only thing she would be hurting was shadows.

You can't fight fire with fire, a voice said inside of her. There was nothing she could do now but shove it to the side. Everyone had seen it: the shadows. Not even Grek had the chance to close his eyes. Despite everything she had sacrificed, their view of her would be forever changed after witnessing her Dark magic.

The image of a little boy wailing at her blackened eyes would stay with her forever.

"Grek! We have to go!" she screamed. After a few desperate tries, she freed herself from the shadow enclosure, but the darkness was still coming. "Grek!" she repeated. "Grek, we have to go!"

Suddenly, an entire chunk of the castle wall fell off, and from the giant hole it left behind, a fifty-foot dragon emerged, covered completely in scarlet scales.

Ez. Oh no. What did he want?

"Coming!" Grek shouted from a pile of rubble. A wall of shadows surrounded her, but a series of flames in quick succession dispersed it. Now, she was *still* trapped, but instead the wall grew bigger, a wall of fire. Grek was on the other side of this wall.

Naomi hauled over a tank of water from the drinks banquet to her right, and poured it over a section of the fire, jumping over before new flames could take its place. She yanked Grek out of the rocky rubble and sighed.

"Ready?"

"You're insane," was all he said.

"Come on. We have to find Heather and Analuna." At that, Grek got up and started running.

"How's my hair?" he said as they were running. Seriously? No wonder Amethyst was always rolling her eyes at him.

"It's fine."

"'Fine?'" he mused, irritated by her comment. "My hair is not just 'fine.' Tales have been told. Legends have been written—"

"It's half burnt and flopping."

That got him to shut up. And thankfully too, because neither her lungs nor her brain could take much more of this conversation. The scene around her did not paint a very pretty picture. Fire and shadows brawled in the palace hall as if it was a wrestling arena, and the few specks of life that still flickered were quickly snuffed out, just like the dead corpses they were weeping over. She was not the artist of this painting. No, merely one of the many brushes used to create it, incapable of shaping its final product. And whoever the artist was, whether it be her mother or some other monster, they painted a cruel, cruel picture indeed.

A shadow shot through her shoulder, flooding her vision with pain.

She hacked out a few coughs, probably from all the smoke and rubble. Her lungs were *killing* her, maybe more than her shoulder. Somehow, though, Grek's lungs seemed to be perfectly fine as he ran alongside her. Naomi lanced him with a puzzled look.

"I guess having lived in the world's most polluted city almost all your life helps for something," he said after her coughs.

Another shadow hit her heel. She just shoved it off with magic and swallowed the pain. It was just a little wound, right? Grek tried to lift her up against him, minimizing her limp, but she pushed him away. "Naomi, c'mon. You're gonna kill yourself like this." Every person in her life had betrayed her. And that was *her* fault.

She let them all get too close.

Grek reached his hand toward her. There it was: friendship, support, safety, *trust.* "Look, Naomi. Urumi and Amethyst must have been saved by the guards. Heather escaped. Everyone's safe."

"Not you," she whispered with another cough. Their world was spinning; she couldn't feel anything but the pain in her lungs, her shoulder, her heel.

"If it weren't for you, Amethyst and I would still be fighting for scraps in Kry."

"I ruined your life."

"No, you gave it back."

Don't trust anyone.

Dear Valaztein, another betrayal would kill her. She wanted to take his hand so badly, just like she'd wanted to open up to Amethyst that day in the cabin. But history had proven that decisions like those could kill her.

Her dad left.

Her mom's shadows bled into her body right now.

Ariah destroyed her only real home.

And Ez... Ez destroyed her.

Don't trust anyone. Don't trust—

Grek leaped in front of her, his body ready to block a spiraling flame. Naomi shoved him away, letting the fire torch her instead. "Why'd you do that?" he shouted.

"Go to the vents with Heather," Naomi replied. "This is my fight, not yours."

"This is *our* fight." Grek reached out his hand once more.

Ez had used those same words. Ariah had promised Naomi friendship too. Her dad had clutched her hand once, swearing he would never let go.

Every single one of them was a liar. Grek would be too.

Don't. Trust. Anyone.

Naomi threw a shadow at Grek, throwing him to the floor faster than he could speak. The voice that came out of her was almost unhuman.

"Go to your sister. Make sure everyone at the vents gets out alright." A tear slid down Naomi's cheek. "Leave. Now."

His eyes glared back at her, stained with hurt. And even worse: stained with fear. She regretted it already, but three seconds later, there was nothing to regret.

A piece of rubble smashed down from the ceiling, knocking the wind out of her. Lights of indigo and crimson danced across the palace hall as far as her eye could see. Pain was all she could feel, all her body *knew how to feel.* Crushed by stone, burned by fire, and pierced by her own mother's shadow, Naomi let out a flood of tears. There was no point in restraining them, because there was no one left to be strong for. And for a moment, she wondered what would kill her first. All the people who had betrayed her—

Or the lack of those she pushed away.

Chapter 27: A Task Long Overdue - (Xouqi Lai)

(Capital) Mae Lì: Northern Province, Tashiki

Xouqi knew this was all his fault. If only all those years ago he—no. There was no time to dwell on the irrevocable, only on that he could salvage.

The fate of his beloved prince.

As he pushed his way through the withered crowd, Xouqi caught sight of a black-and-white-haired girl dressed in a lavender gown. Ah, she was one of the intruders.

"Where is the king?" she asked. The girl pounded on his foot. "I'll repeat, where's the king?"

"Come with me." Xouqi grabbed her arm and continued traversing the wild palace halls. This was perhaps not the response the girl had been expecting, but she made no rash movements. After a few encounters with rogue fire and horrific shadows, they finally reached the clump of guards that surrounded Urumi.

Xouqi sighed. "Guards, take the king to the emergency bunker."

"Through the tunnels?" the commanding officer asked.

"Yes, through the tunnels!"

"What tunnels?" Urumi and the girl both asked.

"They're a highly classified secret."

"I'm the king!" Urumi scoffed, shoving his way out from the clump of guards. Oh, poor boy. If only he knew what had happened in those tunnels years ago... Finally, the guards started moving, and somehow Xouqi and the girl had been pulled into the middle with Urumi.

"What is going on!" the girl demanded.

"Nothing you two have to worry about."

"Nothing we have to worry about?" Urumi repeated. "People are dying! My people!"

"There are things more important than Tashiki, Urumi."

"What things, Lai?" A shadow fired, knocking out one of the guards. He had to keep this under control, to protect Urumi. To protect them all.

"I can't tell you."

"Why, Lai? Why?" Another guard fell, perhaps by another shadow.

"Because she'll do this again!"

"You know who's behind this?!" the girl cut in. They kept arguing with him, but Xouqi had his attention elsewhere. The guards were gone. All twenty-six of them.

"URUMI, RUN!" Zooming ahead, Xouqi led Urumi, his priority, towards the small opening in the ground. The opening that Jiko had made him memorize to the point of perfection. Slamming his hand into the designated space for recognition, he desperately threw off the floor covering and shoved Urumi and the girl down a wooden ladder. All the while, shadow and fire destroyed this once beautiful place of his. Once it was secure, Xouqi jumped into the opening and closed the floor above him.

There, Urumi and the girl were waiting for him, starstruck in this oh, so familiar place.

"Lai, what is this place?" Urumi asked, staring at the slick stone tunnels. The girl looked around and gasped.

"This is the place..." she mumbled.

"Some old offices and an emergency bunker," he lied. There was much more in these walls. Much, much more... "Follow me." They did, and Xouqi grew more anxious by the second. How many had died? Did she succeed? Was the Queen here for Urumi or Jiko's more doomed dedication? Oh, that poor, hidden-away child...

A few minutes later, they reached the bunker. The room was dimly lit and fairly plain. Other than the four beds and bathroom, the room was mostly occupied by food and supplies. This place held so many heart-wrenching memories. It was not a shame that he would never again see this place again. In fact, most things he would not regret after the choice that would be made. Of the people he loved, only one was still alive, and he would be the greatest of all kings. That he would never see that; now that was truly a shame.

"For how long will we be here?" Urumi asked.

"As long as you need to."

"May you please stop speaking in riddles?"

"No, I cannot." The girl had gone off inspecting the room, touching and feeling everything she could. Lai paid little attention to her odd mannerisms.

"What has happened, Lai? What are you trying to protect me from?"

"Not a what, Urumi, a who."

"Does this have anything to do with my father?"

"Quite a bit, yes." Xouqi sighed. This was it. He couldn't stall any longer, or he would not be able to accomplish what needed to be done. "I need you to close your eyes, Urumi."

"Why?"

"Just close your eyes." Urumi did, and Xouqi resisted tears. He slowly backed away, crawling towards the door. By the time Urumi realized what he was doing, it was already too late.

"Lai, stop!" he screamed. "Lai, what are you doing?! You can't leave!"

This was what he had to do, he reminded himself. No matter how much he resisted, this had to be done. And frankly, he was the only one who could do it.

"Goodbye, Urumi."

He locked the door.

Forever.

For always.

For Jiko.

For his best friend's son. For the boy he had come to love. So, when he died, so be it. There was nothing left for him now. His death would tie up the loose ends; protect Urumi until the end of time. With Jiko, Nicholae, and Anaji gone, he was the only thing Miranda could trace back to Urumi. So, he walked through the underground caverns where so many hearts had been shattered, where so many lives had been lost. Blood colored these old, barbaric walls.

In these halls, Anaji had fantasies of snowy creatures.

In these halls, Nicholae dreamed of rebellion.

In these halls, Jiko stole a baby away into the night, protecting it from a fate worse than death.

Yes, this was a task long overdue.

And now, the hard part was over. This was how fate would have it, because he did not feel afraid. More, rejuvenated. Was this how someone knew they were ready? He climbed up that ladder with a newfound understanding, one that would finally allow him to release this burden. All the while hearing his best friend and his former king's words.

Protect my son, Xouqi. Protect my son.

A shadow plunged his heart, sealing the past away forever.

Chapter 28: Those Emerald Green Eyes - (Ez)

(Capital) Mae Lì: Northern Province, Tashiki

Ez soared across the smoking sky, adrenaline rushing through his body, almost letting him forget who he was. In the distance, a kingdom crumbled. The palace, which had looked so threatening in all its warish glory, now looked, well, pathetic. Just a bunch of reckless royals destroying a symbol. Miranda should've raided the armory instead.

Ez had never been one for the idealistic.

Was that what made him so… cold? Maybe if he could just fix his screwed-up brain, he could stop ruining everyone's lives. Including Naomi's, which probably would've ended in that palace if he'd arrived any later. What was she thinking, sending the rest of her little gang off while she practically died on the floor? The honey-haired boy (who also remained unconscious on Ez's back) had been the only other person left alive amidst the wreckage.

The thought sent a shiver down his spine. A very familiar shiver.

He waited for that pang of guilt that should come after a massacre like this one, but his stomach didn't turn at all. *What's another thousand or so?* a voice in his mind whispered. Most days he wanted to murder that little voice, scream until his ears bled. Other days, he felt like that voice was all he was. If the violent, bruised, stone-hearted part of him was gone, what the heck was left?

And on the worst days, he didn't care. He didn't care if killing the voice would kill him, too. It wouldn't be so bad... at least he would stop hurting everyone.

All he had to do was keep it together for a little longer. Patch up Naomi and her friend, leave them with supplies enough to fight the cold, and then disappear. Of course he wanted to stay with her, hold her, make sure she wasn't hurt anymore by an unforgiving world. But it wasn't the world that hurt Naomi.

It was him.

His choice. His unbreakable, unchangeable human nature. From the day he killed his parents in that blood-soaked carriage, Ez had begun to craft a very broken kid. Everything he'd ever been through had made him this way: an eye for an eye, kill or be killed.

Those few months with Naomi had been the best in his life, because he felt himself change. He felt Naomi *changing* him. Every moment with her was one where his past didn't cling to his heart like a parasite.

But they were both idiots.

One girl couldn't undo nearly two decades of pain. There was no amount of love that could heal a heart that didn't exist, not that he was deserving of it anyway. Poor Daunt... Ez had put him in danger countless times too. Just like Naomi, he would learn that Ez was a bomb ready to blow. Ez knew that someday he would hurt that kid, and no one would forgive him. Cause sooner or later everyone would see what Naomi saw, what Miranda *knew*:

Just how much of a monster he was.

Once he arrived, Ez wasted no time. Quickly, he transformed back into a person and laid out Naomi and the other man on the grass. All of this he did while ignoring Daunt's constant prodding, frustrating as it was.

"Daunt, I need you to grab me as many leaves as you can, okay?" He scurried off. Grabbing his canteen, Ez started pouring water on each of their wounds. Never before was he so grateful for that utterly tedious class Infitri gave on healing Dark magic wounds. He continued pouring water on the wounds until Daunt finally arrived with an armful of leaves.

"Is this good?"

"Yeah. Now you have to go to the bunker store we passed by and get me a medicine that says 'Crackel Heal', okay?" Daunt nodded.

"Got it." Ez handed him some gold that he had stolen back in the Eastern Province. Thankfully, the store was nearby, so Daunt should be back soon. For now, he just kept pouring water onto the wounds. Once Naomi and the man next to her seemed to be breathing alright, he proceeded to use the leaves Daunt had brought him. After mashing them for a while, the leaves were reduced to a brownish mush, which he quickly applied to their wounds.

Oh, what a disaster.

Then, all he could do was wait anxiously for Daunt to arrive with the medicine.

Frustration started kicking in, and he found himself hitting at a blossom tree.

"Come on, Daunt. Come on." A few minutes later, Daunt did arrive, and with a generous amount of medicine.

"Is this it?"

"Yes."

And with that, he got to work. Removing the bandage of leaves, Ez started applying the gel-like medicine on the open wounds. Daunt stood ready with extra water. He didn't waste a heartbeat after he finished applying the medicine. Daunt collected some moss, and they propped both of them down on the grass in what he hoped was a comfortable position. He and Daunt then covered them with some of their camping blankets. Obviously a hospital would have been ideal, but ideal didn't seem to be playing a very large role in his life anymore.

He only realized his frail companion's condition a few minutes later.

"Ez," Daunt said, his teeth chattering. "It's cold."

"Just a few minutes longer, Daunt. Just a few minutes longer." He could feel the little boy shivering.

"Are they ever going to wake up?"

"Yeah. They're going to wake up really soon."

Oh, how he hoped he wasn't lying.

A few hours later, Ez felt more and more like he *had* lied. Daunt was shivering ferociously, and neither Naomi nor the man who had been protecting her had moved. The only signs of life were a faint pulse and a weak breath. He willed himself not to collapse into a broken heap.

"I'm cold, Ez. I'm cold."

"I know you're cold. You just gotta hang on, okay?"

"You know what would help me hang on better?" he said.

"What?"

"A story."

"Oh no."

"Oh, yes. Or I'm gonna snatch that blanket right off of that pretty lady over there."

After a quick eye roll, Ez replied, "Fine. What kind of story do you want?"

"A happy one."

"Alright. Once there was a princess."

"Once upon a *time*, Ez. You have very bad storytelling skills." He chuckled. Well, as much as he could without forming ice on his tongue.

"Once upon a time, there was a princess. And she lived in a far-off kingdom, trapped in a gloomy palace. Her mother, the cruelest queen ever to live, was forcing her to marry someone she did not want to marry. So, she escaped the palace, found adventure, and saved her kingdom from scary magic. And she lived happily ever after. The end."

"But I wanna hear *your* story, Ez." Daunt shivered again.

"Well, that one doesn't have such a neat happily ever after."

"I still wanna hear it!"

"Maybe another time, deal?"

"Okay, deal." Ez rubbed his hands through Daunt's short dreadlocks. "Stop! You're cold!" Ez just grinned, holding in a laugh.

"Got it."

"It's not funny!"

"Never change, Daunt. Never, ever change." Daunt looked confused, but he would understand once he grew up. Speaking of growing up...

Ez walked over and gazed at Naomi. Her lips were stained by the cold, glossed by a layer of winter frost. Her dazzling palace gown reminded him of how things used to be, before their worlds flipped. Snowflakes glittered in her dark hair, just like they had in Rellen, back when they were on a mission to save Valaztein.

Naomi would always be beautiful to him, whether she was covered in scars or consumed by shadows. She shivered, and Ez wrapped his jacket around her. Memories of holding her in his arms came flooding back, one by one. But he had to let them go.

He had to let *her* go.

Protecting Naomi from Miranda was impossible, but at least Ez could protect her from himself. Things would never return to the way they were, and the sooner he let go of the guy he wanted to be, the better.

He was scarred.

He was broken.

He was dangerous.

Ez worked alone, because his past would come back to haunt everyone he loved. So, no matter how his heart burned, he had to stop loving Naomi.

"Let's go," Ez told Daunt.

"Shouldn't we stay until they wake up?"

"No," Ez replied. "They wouldn't want to see me anyway."

"Why? You saved their lives."

"Just trust me." Ez's heart burned as he said the words. Daunt was the kid he could've been: sweet, compassionate, innocent. And every day, Daunt put all his trust in Ez, ready to believe his every word.

One would think that the bruise on the kid's throat would've changed his mind.

Ez was no saint. And he was no big brother. That day in the carriage was enough proof of that. That's why he had to find the dragon heir. If he didn't find it, if he didn't save his race... then all this would've been for nothing.

"I'll always trust you, Ez." Daunt's voice was quiet in the cold, almost unheard amidst the storm in Ez's mind. "You save people. Someone wanted you to meet me. They knew I needed a guardian angel. They knew you needed a compass, too."

"You're just a kid; you don't know what you're talking about."

Daunt hid a sheepish grin. "Neither do you," he replied.

"Excuse me?" Ez's patience for this conversation was withering with every shiver.

"You put your jacket around that girl over there." Freaking shivers! "You wouldn't have done that if you didn't want her to know that you saved her life."

"She was cold."

"So are you." Daunt's observations were as easy to spot as they were painful to hear. He was being lectured by a ten-year-old.

"It was the right thing to do," Ez snapped.

"Yeah, just like when you tried to kill me with a knife the first time we met." Daunt rolled his eyes while he said it, that kiddish smirk ever present.

"Look, I'm getting cold and tired of this conversation." Ez pushed his way past Daunt, beginning to mutter his incantation. "Flem—"

"Then take your jacket back."

"No."

"Why?" Daunt insisted.

"'Cause I don't want her to die of cold!"

"You know, I think leaving her alone outside in a freezing winter is really going to help with that."

"Zip it, kid."

"What voices in your head are *so* important that you have to shush everyone around you?"

The words hit him like a punch to the gut. Ez turned around, eyes set aflame.

"Demons," Ez whispered. "Try killing your whole family. You'll want the whole damn world to shut up, too. Still think I'm your angel now?"

Daunt stepped back, silent. For once, no words shot out of his little mouth. Standing there, his skin covered in snow, he looked like a doll. Small. Easy to break.

But that childlike smile was gone. And stunning Daunt out of words didn't make the voices inside of Ez any quieter.

Liar. Killer. Traitor. Monster.

Where had the world gone? Daunt's tapping feet, the whistle of the wind, the shivers in his spine… Anything was better than his thoughts. Anything was better than the silence. The people he'd lost, ran away from, betrayed, and killed, flooded through his mind. Ariah's tears as she let go of his hand. Naomi's eyes, blackened by shadows. Daunt's fragile body, shuddering in the cold. The silence was worse than anything he'd ever known.

And then a piercing scream broke through the air.

Ez dropped his satchel and sprinted towards Naomi. Even when sleeping, she couldn't be free of her pain… Even though her eyes were shut she still screamed and sobbed like Miranda was beside her.

People like that never stop haunting you, whether your eyes are open or closed. Ez lifted her up, holding her tight against him.

"I'm here, Naomi," he said. "You're safe. I promise, she can't hurt you here." Naomi grasped his wrist, her screams stopping. Relief rushed through him as Naomi began to feel safe.

Maybe she'd never truly be safe, but for this moment, in his arms, nothing would hurt her. "I love you," he whispered, so quiet not even the gods could hear him. "I loved you then and I'll love you for the rest of my life, Princess."

As the silence crept in, Ez wasn't afraid anymore. Because this was real. More real than the voices in his head or the memories plaguing his heart. Daunt was right; shutting everyone out leaves you with only the voices in your head. No matter how loud, no matter how real... they could never be more important than the voices of the people beside him. Of Naomi. Of Daunt, who now hugged him in a tight embrace.

"You're an idiot," Daunt said. "One day you'll understand that there's not a thing in this world that could change what I know is true about you. I don't care who you were, Ez. And I know you were hurt, but look, you still have people in this world who you care about. You don't know what it's like to be alone. I mean, *really* alone. You have to understand, you're the only person in my life who hasn't hurt me or left me. You're a good person. And you're everything to me."

Daunt was a boy well-versed in loneliness. For years, this little kid had lived in his head, in his memories, in his pain. And somehow... he'd overcome his demons. He'd been loud enough that the voices silenced.

Ez had been alone twice before. Once when he lost his family. The next when he lost his race. Ariah's death marked the end of that world. She was cruel, deceitful, and broken... but they were lonely together. Two faces of the same monster. Because traitors pay.

In loss.

In heartache.

In blood.

But if he could make such a difference in Daunt's life, then being alone wasn't an option anymore. This was a different kind of family. Not of blood, not of scales... but of hope. Of screwed-up kids done with giving up. Cast out, orphaned, hunted, and heartbroken, but not done.

No more hidden escapes. No more masked faces. No more witch queens.

Long live the rebellion.

CHAPTER 29: PRIDE AND PAIN - (AMETHYST)

(Capital) Mae Lì: Northern Province, Tashiki

Amethyst pounded at the door.

"Let us out, old man!" Uh, this was *not* happening! She and Grek had gone chasing after a fairytale: a pretty princess who promised rags to riches. And where did that leave her?

Here. In a dusty bunker screaming at a stone door. Oh, and how could she forget the prince into whose arms she had just cleverly fallen into? Everything was wrong. This wasn't her life; it never had been! What an idiot… to think something so perfect could last.

Urumi looked blankly at the room. His suit grimy, his body trembling in the corner where he lay. The calm king-in-waiting was gone. This Urumi was unrecognizable. After his dimpled smile had been wiped away, the only things left were cold eyes and a croaking whisper.

"Amethyst, stop—" he said.

"We can do this!"

"He's gone, just—"

"I don't care!" Amethyst replied as she snatched a pin from Urumi's hair and started picking the lock. Why wasn't it working? This should be so easy, it should be second nature!

Urumi grabbed her hand, pulling it away from the door.

"It's done!" he said. "There's nothing we can do." Amethyst had never seen him like this before: defeated, hopeless, heartbroken.

"Urumi, we can fix this. Together."

"You don't get it. It was *my* coronation that got wrecked, remember? My future!" he snapped. Why was he doing this? Why was he being such a jerk?

"We *do* have a future. You taught me that. Don't let your past ruin it. Your mom wouldn't have wanted that."

"My people are dying out there, Amethyst!" he yelled. "I wouldn't expect you to understand how that feels."

"Gods, if you could *hear* how entitled you sound! Everything and everyone I've ever loved is out there."

"Are you seriously comparing your squad of delinquent thieves to an entire kingdom?"

"At least my family doesn't live under tombstones!" Amethyst spat out. The words came out faster than she could stop them. And oh, how she wished she could.

"You know what? I'm sorry. I'm sorry I kissed you. I'm sorry I ever met you at all."

Amethyst stared at him, every bone in her body trying not to believe him.

"You don't mean that."

"Of course I do! You ruined my life! If it weren't for you and your friends, the shadows wouldn't even be here. You: a thief, a nobody." He wiped the sweat dripping onto his forehead. "You made me into my father."

"Oh, you never needed my help with that. You're just as much of a jackass as he was," she replied, pushing away tears with screams. That was enough. She'd tried to be supportive, kind… but that was it. "I'm such an idiot; I really thought people like you could change! Because for a minute there you made me believe that I was good enough. For you. For this." Amethyst looked up, picturing herself in a beautiful ball gown, waving at a cheering kingdom with Urumi by her side.

An image that would never come true.

She jabbed the pin into the lock, finally focusing on the flicks of her fingers and the clicking of the door. It sort of gave her déjà vu. In a way, picking a lock helped her remember who she was:

A thief.

A nobody.

Penniless.

Not good enough for a prince.

The door clicked open and Urumi went rushing through it. Spots appeared in her vision as his body turned into merely a princely silhouette sprinting into the distance. Amethyst couldn't run the way he did. Because Urumi was running to save his home. A thing she would never have.

And also because the world turned black before she got three feet out the door.

Chapter 30: Valiant Dreams of Death and Martyrs — (Urumi)

(Capital) Mae Lì: Northern Province, Tashiki

Urumi rushed back towards Amethyst the moment he heard her gasp, catching her just before she hit the ground. No, no, no!

"Amethyst, Amethyst, wake up," he said while shaking her. "Please, please, you can't leave me here alone."

He kept shaking and kept screaming, but Amethyst made not a single sound. For every moment he spent in the damp tunnels, her skin turned colder. This girl wasn't waking up anytime soon. And from the looks of it, Urumi wasn't getting out of these tunnels soon either.

In ten minutes, his world had turned from the vibrant hues of the coronation to endless shades of gray. His entire life was gone. Everything.

All because of him. And his fascination with a girl he could never marry anyway.

Wiping away sweat or tears (who could tell now), Urumi stumbled over to the bunker and slung a satchel full of rations over his shoulder. Memories burst through his mind as he began a journey through the tunnels with Amethyst in his arms.

Memories of the good times.

Being curled up beside his parents, flipping through fables in a quiet library nook. His mom's smile as she kissed his dad. The way they both waved at Tashiki from the palace balcony, as if nothing mattered more than that moment, those people. The limitless love in his father's eyes as he gazed at his wife, who was giggling at the newest extravagant gala. He did everything to protect her. To protect his family. Until he couldn't.

And then there were the bad times.

The maid who delivered the news with tears in her eyes. The lock on his father's door that shut away everything and everyone for years, even his own son. The messages coming in from countries all over, competing to manipulate the heartbroken king of Tashiki; the victor remained a mystery to Urumi. The coldness in his dad's eyes, as if the world had lost its color. Because it had. To Urumi's father, a life without his wife simply wasn't one worth living. A kingdom without its queen wasn't worth protecting. And a son without his mom would never be enough of a family.

His dad should've kept it together. Why? Why did he let himself love his mom so much that he had no love left once she was gone?

It wasn't fair. Tashiki bore the weight of its king's broken heart. And Tashiki bore that weight once more today, because Urumi fell in love with someone too. Tashiki was the price to pay for a lifetime filled with her snarky jokes and curled smile. Perhaps a boy could entertain such fantasies, but that little prince was washed away today by the blood of thousands. And that blood left a mark, one that reminded him of who he was now. Who he had to be for Tashiki.

A king who held his heart close to his chest.

A king who could never fall in love.

Time lost its meaning in those tunnels. Days, hours... they were all the same in the end. His arms were sore from hauling Amethyst with him and his mind was tired of the endless circles he seemed to be walking in. Urumi thought of everything in the time that passed: Amethyst, his parents, Tashiki. It was funny how the very things that tormented him were also the ones that kept him going.

Step by painful step.

And after marking every trail he'd already attempted and peeking through every crevice and bunker to be found, Urumi saw his way out. A wooden hatch led to a whole new tunnel system, smaller and darker. It took nearly a day of crawling on his knees for the light to appear.

Fickle, tiny, but a light all the same.

So, he kept dragging himself through, Amethyst in toe, until the little light became a grand opening and the opening became a scene filled with daylight.

His eyes squinted at the world around him, once again blooming with color and life. Sunshine shimmered over the cottony snow sprinking gold across the little garden where Urumi now stood. Oh, but it was no ordinary garden. No, in this very place, stood his mother's grave.

Blossoms of periliths and dillies curled around a casket, springing from the frost in all their beauty. *Evergreen flowers.* Stubborn and stunning, just like his mom. Nature framed its queen, who lay in a crystal casket protected from time by sorcery. Before his father's death, Urumi would make the long walk from the palace to his mother's grave every day, and every day she appeared identical. Long, flowing auburn hair pinned back by pearls and freckled cheeks the color of spring lilies. One day, he would walk to his mom's grave older than she would ever be.

Time took Urumi's mother.

And He was never giving her back.

The only thing left of her was this quiet grave, and it was the only thing his father refused to let crumble after his mom's death. Every feature of it reminded Urumi of his mom. The checkered marble floor was like the chessboard where they competed, even though it was never much of a contest. The book lying open in her hands was—

Wait. There was a page of the novel bookmarked. That was new. It must have been placed there after his father's death.

A message from his dead dad hidden in his mother's grave. If it weren't so close to home, he would've chuckled at the orphan cliche. And yet Urumi's happiness was short-lived, because another thought made its way into his head: there was no sorcerer with him. No one to maintain the time spell while he grabbed the book. If he wanted to read his father's message, Urumi would have to—

No. How could he even fathom such an idea? Why would he desecrate his mother's grave just to read some message from his good-for-nothing father? His dad *chose* to leave. He chose to give up on his kingdom and on his son. Urumi would make no such mistake.

And then he saw Amethyst. Her crazy hair, wild smile, and pain-stained words. Words that meant more coming from her than from any queen.

"We do have a future. Don't let your past ruin it.
Your mom wouldn't have wanted that."

And Amethyst was right. Urumi had been so afraid of becoming his father, of letting love control him… that he'd forgotten who he was. Shutting out anyone who cared about him wouldn't make him a better king. His love wasn't a flaw, it was the very thing that would save him from a reign of cruelty. Maybe his dad's love was a cautionary tale… but maybe it didn't have to be. To change his future, really *truly* change its course, he had to let go of his parents' pain.

So he smashed his mother's casket.

The crystal shattered within a second, spiraling off across the garden chamber. Urumi snatched the book, tucking it under his shoulder as he reached for his mom's hand. It was cold, *so* cold. He gazed at her face one last time, taking in every crease and lift, every scar and smile line. Urumi looked at her until his eyes couldn't take it any longer, witnessing how time slowly turned her bones to ash. Finally, he blinked.

And she was gone.

Urumi shivered in the merciless winter, clutching a book to his side, utterly alone. Willing away tears, he flipped the novel open to the newly bookmarked page. Neatly tucked in that page lay a letter, palace-sealed and perfect.

Dear Urumi,
If you're reading this letter, I'm dead.

Whoa, what a way for his dad to ease him in. Urumi read on.

And if you're reading this, all the apologies in the world won't change your view of me, so I will not try. Your mother didn't die in a time gap. If she had, you wouldn't be standing at her grave now. She was killed by Queen Miranda, murdered in the dead of night by beasts of shadow. You were just a child, but Miranda sent shadows to kill you too, lurking under your bed, following your every footstep. Miranda made me a deal: I gave her Tashiki or she took you.

I had no choice. You are Tashiki's only heir, and beyond that... you're my son.

I write this letter on your birthday, pill in hand. As much as I hate to leave you, you're old enough for the throne. Tashiki will spend not a day longer than it needs under Miranda's blackmail. Perhaps as you read this, you are already a king, and no doubt, you will be a better one than I ever was.

And yet, I do not regret a thing. I loved you and your mother more than anything, and in the end, I lost you both. For years, all I could feel was the pain. But pain is just a reminder that you're alive. And I'd live a thousand lives with that pain just to live one with my family.

I loved your mother. And I love you.
And no amount of pain will ever change that.

Sincerely,
Dad

Chapter 31: Shattered - (Naomi)

(Capital) Mae Lì: Northern Province, Tashiki

Naomi felt the shadows consuming her, slithering from her boots to her waist to her chest.

Chained to the ground, Naomi could see Miranda above her, as elegant and untouched as ever.

She lay in a black dungeon. No fire, no light. In fact, the room was freezing.

"Let the shadows take you, Naomi. Let them take away the pain." Miranda walked out of the room, heels clattering against the metal floor as she locked the door.

"Help!" Naomi screamed. "Please, someone!"

Her father walked in, chestnut eyes and ruffled hair. He was dressed the same as the day he left: blue coat, stiff boots, and no crown.

"I have to go, Tulip," he whispered in her ear. "I have to save Valaztein."

"Save me," she sobbed. "Save me, Dad."

And then he was gone. It was just her and the shadows. They crept up to her neck, stealing the breath from her lungs and the blood from her veins. With every passing second, her world turned darker and colder.

No one was coming to save her. Miranda was right about the shadows. It's easier to break than to get broken. And it's easier to be a traitor than to be betrayed. She gasped for air, but it wouldn't come. She stared at the door, praying to see someone. Anyone. If only she'd listened to her friends... If only she hadn't pushed them away...

I'm here, Naomi.

The voice was a whisper, but stronger. Naomi wasn't alone.

You're safe. I promise she can't hurt you here.

The chains disappeared. The shadows too. The cold stopped as arms tightened around her. The rhythm of a heartbeat flooded her mind, steady and slow.

I love you, said the voice. *I loved you then and I'll love you for the rest of my life, Princess.*

The walls shattered like glass. Voices mumbled around her as the world spun. With a gasp, her eyes shot open. Sunlight flooded in, reflected across the snow and trees. A little kid played in the barren bushes near her, making angels in the snow. The cold air, the feeling of frost below her... this was real.

And so was Ez.

His midnight black hair, his crystal blue eyes. His lips, trickled with frost and daring her to kiss them.

"You saved my life," she muttered, not really believing the words herself.

"Naomi, I—"

"You betrayed me. You betrayed Valaztein. Why save me now?" Gosh, even his coat was wrapped around her! She slipped it off and threw it against the snow. Her arms burned as she did, a reminder of the coronation and the shadows.

"Because I'm done being Miranda's pawn."

"Why the heck should I believe you?"

"You shouldn't. I wouldn't believe me either," he replied. Naomi squeezed her hands, hating his snide remarks and loving them at the same time. She should've walked away, left Ez behind like the traitor that he was. But there was one question that couldn't go unanswered. One question that had haunted her soul since the day she escaped the Maze.

"Why, Ez?"

"It doesn't make up for anything."

"No more lies. No more excuses," Naomi replied. "You owe me that much."

"There's this thing spoken about for centuries in dragon lore: a person whose blood can revive the dragon race. An heir. I struck a deal with Miranda for its location. Valaztein in exchange for the dragon heir."

Now she knew. Ez was still that kid from the streets of Milu. Loyal to his dragons like Naomi was to Valaztein. Country before love... that's the choice he made. Maybe he was right to have made it, but it still hurt. Ez continued, "I escaped to find the dragon heir. I was so close, but when I learned about the attack on the palace... I had to come find you. I made a deal with the devil—"

"And I was your price," Naomi filled in.

"Miranda told me you were dead."

"Sometimes I wish I was." The words came quietly, like a trickling creek that floods into a booming waterfall. Naomi sat in silence for nearly a minute, waiting for Ez to say something, anything.

"I know the feeling."

"That's not fair," she shot back. "You don't get to feel sorry for yourself."

"You don't know what it's like to lose you, Princess." *Princess.* All her life she'd been called that, in honor and in disdain. But Ez said it differently. Funny to think that regardless of how complicated things got, one word made everything simple again.

"*I* know what it's like to lose you," she spat. "You gave me away." She paced around in the snow, angry at the way her heels sunk and her body shivered. Angry at Ez. Angry at the world. "But I don't care about that anymore. I *can't* care about that anymore. Life goes on without us. But you gave away our home."

"*Our* home?" Ez replied. "I'm sorry that I don't have too much love for a country that has hunted and destroyed my kind for thousands of years. A country that killed my parents and my real home."

"You know what? I'm done fighting." Naomi's voice broke as she said it, but the words were true. Fleeing to Tashiki, traveling with thieves, begging for help from a heartbroken prince... what good had that led to? More deaths. More pain. More heartbreak. "I'm done trying to save the kingdom and I'm done trusting people like you. I've suffered enough for my country."

"The girl I know would never say that."

"What a surprise, two years in hell can change someone!" Naomi slapped him hard across the cheek. "Thank you for saving my life. Now get out of here. And don't come near me again unless you want more than a mark on your face."

"No."

"No?" she spat out.

"You can't stop fighting." He grabbed her hand, steady and strong.

"Watch me." Naomi snapped her hand away and stared into his eyes. Her gaze intensified as she waited for him to look away.

"And you'll never suffer enough for your country. You'll suffer and suffer and suffer some more until you win or die. It's who you are."

"Well, forgive me for not wanting that," she said.

"So what's your great plan, huh? Never trust anyone ever again?"

"Better than constantly being used." Naomi sighed, shaky in the cold. "I'm not an idiot, okay? I know I'll never get the fairy tale or the white prince or any of that. But I don't want my life to sum up to dates on a history book or a cautionary tale about the princess who died at seventeen."

A feeling in her gut told her that she was doing the wrong thing, that she was letting everyone down. But why was the world hers to carry? Most of her family was dead and the only person remaining was trying to kill her! Wasn't it better to be alone than betrayed? "I don't care how many times you save me, Ez. I will *never* forgive you. This is the last time I let a jerk like you hurt me."

"When your precious Valaztein is in ruins, I won't be the one you can't forgive." And then he finally broke her gaze and walked away. "Daunt, let's go."

The jitters in her stomach grew until she could barely feel herself. This shouldn't feel so wrong! She was right to let Ez go. She deserved to be happy. And yet Ez's words still shook her core. Valaztein shouldn't pay for her screwed-up childhood or her parents' mistakes. Two years ago, she had made a promise after her sister's death. And repeated it after Gin was taken. And after Infitri's death.

I'll fight because you can't. I'll fight for the Valaztein we dreamed about.

Back when she didn't know pain or betrayal like this. Back when she'd seen people be hurt but never been hurt herself. And if she turned her back on that promise… this feeling would only grow.

I'll fight for this future.

That's what she told herself after every heartbreak. The truth about her father, Gin's death, the dragon massacre, the bombing at Eppeye… all of it. She survived because there was still a dawn waiting to break. But now the sun was nowhere in sight, and even if it was, Naomi was in no position to see it.

Was she still willing to risk everything for that future? For freedom and love and peace?

Could she live with herself if she didn't?

"Ez," Naomi called out. "Stay."

Chapter 32: The Girl With No Past - (Amethyst)

(Capital) Mae Lì: Northern Province, Tashiki

Amethyst awoke in a vision. It was the same experience: drowning, reemerging, having the world flipped and making it onto the bridge. When she got to the bridge, though, it was different.

One-quarter of the way through, halfway, three quarters. She waited to take another step. Had she ever been this far before? No, she decided. No, she had not. So, she took another step, and another, and another, and another. The bridge never collapsed, and an invisible force never pulled her down. It was the strangest sensation.

Before she knew it, Amethyst was five steps away from reaching the other side. Now, she could see that on the other side stood a door. A blackened wood door with a silver handle. She inhaled. Why was this so wrong? Why did reaching the end of the Crossing feel so… unnatural?

She exhaled. One step. Breathe in. Two steps. Breathe out. Three steps. Breathe in. Four steps. Breathe out.

All of this happened without falling. She just kept walking and walking and walking. How? Well, all she knew was that there was one step left to cross the Crossing. This was it.

Breathe in. Five steps.

This moment was when she would fall. But she didn't.

Amethyst was walking on air. Pure, somehow sturdy, air. She could turn in any direction, but she chose the door. Well, it's not like there was much else to walk to. Once she reached it and twisted the knob, it flew right open. The moment she walked through it, now that was when she started falling. And screaming.

The fall was even longer than her usual. It felt like all eternity had gone by as she fell, and even worse, her surroundings were pitch black. What a horrible way to get her bearings. Finally, she reached a stop. She was in a beautifully decorated living room, or at least, it would have been beautiful if not for the fact that everything was floating in midair.

There sat a gorgeous woman with light brown skin, emerald green eyes, blood-red lips, and a golden crown. Whispers echoed in Amethyst's mind: *this is someone to fear.* This woman was not floating in the blank abyss that Amethyst was, but instead, lying comfortably on an imperial throne.

"Good morning, Amethyst. I'm Queen Miranda of Valaztein, or as you know me, Miri." What? This was Miri? "Oh, my apologies." She zapped a chair out of its non-gravitational state and flicked Amethyst into it. She found that she couldn't move, not even an inch. "Much more comfortable, correct?"

"Why are you here?"

"The same reason you are," she replied. "Because I need to be."

"What do you mean?"

"Let's start at the beginning, shall we? Of course, I'd love to return the three years of memories they stole from you, but Infitri's magic is irreversible. Trust me, Amethyst, I've tried."

"Who's Infitri? Why do you know my name?"

"It all began years ago, a few after dear Ez was born."

"Who's—"

"Your brother." Wait, some of it was coming back. "You too were in a beautiful golden carriage, provided by yours truly, to bring you to sanctuary at my palace. Just then, the wretched boy killed his two parents, *your* parents, but left you to my mercy."

She gasped. Blood. Flesh. Ice-blue eyes. Scales. Why scales?

"I remember."

"I, terrified by the insanity of the six-year-old's cruelty, took you under my wing. I protected you, cared for you."

A spiked chair, darkness, shadows, emerald-green eyes.

"There's something you aren't telling me." Amethyst tried to move out of the chair, but this weird reality hindered her escape. "What did you do to me?!" The chair restrained her every move, almost choking her to death.

"Oh fine, some of my experiments might've... discomforted you along the way, but that's how you got your powers." Amethyst halted in her struggle. All this time, scrambling for an answer and this was the hard, cold truth. She was worse than some common peasant; she was a... toy, a lab rat for people like Miranda to do with as they pleased.

"What?"

"I tampered with Dark and black magic, slowly combining the two to create the weapon you are today."

"I'm not a weapon."

"Correct, you're *my* weapon. But anyways, your strange hair resulted from a few of my failed attempts and so did your thick-headedness, apparently."

"How dare you—" Miranda lifted a finger and her mouth closed. How could this be real? How could those horrible men in Kry, the filthy rich who took pleasure in insulting her, be right?

"I created this place, Amethyst. Wouldn't I know how to manipulate it?" She sighed. "Back to what I was telling you. You were my little experiment, a bomb that I'd be able to drop anywhere I wanted. I developed your powers, Amethyst, and not just the ones you're aware of."

"Like what?"

"Why do you think the Time Gaps were only in the Southern Province?"

"I don't know."

"Because you *are* the time gaps, Amethyst. Every time you use your powers, a time gap follows. That's why they spread to the Northern Province. That's why you're a danger to everyone around you. That bracelet on your wrist was meant to be a tracker, but that horrid dragon magic turned it to gibberish. Seems your brother was able to find you after stealing my amulet, because he's been following you for months."

"Why?"

Miranda grinned. "Don't you worry, darling; it's nothing of importance."

"No, this can't—"

"Sadly, my pathetic husband found you when you were just a baby and stole you away to the wretched Southern Province."

"How did you find me?"

"Because I learned how to control you. Along with your mind."

"That's impossible,"

Miranda smirked. It all seemed so stupid now. When she was a kid, she could still dream of what her life could've been. Back then it seemed that maybe her parents were nobles or well-respected countryfolk. But no. She was just a pawn to the rich and powerful, and Miranda made it crystal clear that that was all she would ever be.

"Oh really? What about your visions? Why do you think I give you those?"

"I don't know."

"To communicate with you, Amethyst. And as I clearly have shown you, they aren't fake."

"So, you can read the future?"

"No, dear. Your powers can. I just choose what you see. Think of it as a thank you."

"No. It's a way to manipulate my mind." Amethyst gritted her teeth. How was this possible? Uh, why had she listened to Grek back in Kry? This whole mess began because she let herself believe that any of this could change! Now all she wanted was to go back and tell herself to stay in that miserable little town. And the cruelest thing? Hope.

Hope hurts more than any feeling in the world. At least in Kry, Amethyst *knew* she was worthless. Here, she had to learn it all over again. After miles and miles and miles of traveling, after kissing a prince for crying out loud... Amethyst was *still* worthless. Well, who was she kidding? A couple weeks of travel and one kiss wouldn't make the world turn upside down. People like Urumi, Miranda, or Naomi... those are the people that decide value. A prince thought she was pretty, not smart. And why should she expect anything more than that?

Maybe it was time to stop clawing at the idea of respect.

Maybe it was time to stop dreaming of being a lady of the court, a hero, or a queen.

Maybe it was time to accept that all she would ever be was a princess's friend, a queen's pawn, and a girl too pathetic for a king.

Today Amethyst said goodbye to that little girl's dreams, because this was the reality: she wasn't enough and would never be.

"See it as you'd like. But try not to kill that new friend of yours; torturing her corpse wouldn't be as fun as a live Naomi. And tell me when you kill Grek. I'll make him a pretty coffin."

"You witch! You'l—"

"Goodbye, Amethyst. See you in your dreams."

When Amethyst woke up, Urumi was hovering above her, concern, relief, and compassion all flooding his blue eyes. No, she couldn't think about Urumi anymore, about anything.

"Urumi, you have to kill me."

A Teaser for the Next Book in

The Shadow Heir Trilogy...

In a dark chamber, a king mourned. For what in this world was there left to live for? All that remained of his love were two clueless children and a few ashes, yet an entire kingdom awaited his heartfelt speech about perseverance in the face of grief.

The shadow of the iron lantern adjacent to him lengthened until it was the size of a person. From it emerged a queen. Her emerald green eyes glittered in the darkness; glaring, and piercing, and destroying wherever they landed. Unfortunately for him, they had settled nearby—a death sentence for any living creature. The queen wore a viridescent gown, and raven-black tresses intertwined with lively jewels cascaded down her back. Her crimson lips opened, but the king spoke first.

"You are a trespasser, a witch, unwelcome and unwanted in a land free of black spells."

"I have come to make you a deal, as formal as that of any other," she responded.

"And what is this groundbreaking offer, may I ask?" The lantern abruptly flickered into the midnight gloom, leaving them in darkness.

"There is a war coming, Deimos, and I need Lightmoon's support," the queen said. "*Military* support."

"And how would you know of this upcoming war?"

"I created it."

"Of course you did," he answered, sighing. "And what would be given in return?"

"Other than my mercy?" The king's face turned grim and weary, appalled by the long night to come. The queen burst out laughing. "I am only joking. Can a queen not have a sense of humor?"

"What do you want, Miranda?"

"Now that is no way to address your future sovereign, is it? All I want is to give you the only thing you've ever truly desired. Your wife." Just as he was about to object, Miranda snapped her fingers and materialized a tenebrous mirror.

"Where did you get this?" he demanded.

"I stole it from a little girl," she replied with a smirk. "You get it once a day. Thirty minutes." Suddenly, the glossy surface of the mirror turned to murky water, like ink, and there appeared the reflection of his wife.

"You will not manipulate me with your magic. Dark magic is strictly banned!"

"Perhaps. But I know you, Deimos. You have pulled more than a few strings to protect your family, so why not now?"

"She is dead." Yet the reflection of his wife still called to him, luring his grieving spirit through the mirror.

"Go into the mirror. I will pull you out in thirty minutes." His heart ached to follow the instructions, but his conscience knew better. Still... would he ever have this chance again? No, no he wouldn't. Just as the queen intended, he walked into the mirror, his fractured mind offering little resistance against his yearning heart.

Acknowledgments

There are so many people without whom this series would not be possible, and I am infinitely grateful for all of them.

Firstly, I'd like to thank my family for always being so supportive of my work. Every day, I rush down to dinner to read them the latest chapter of my newest book, and they always listen with open ears. *Los amo muchísimo*: Grego, Sari, Mami, Dadda, Yuyi, y Abue.

A big thank you to the entire team responsible for bringing this book to life: Chris, my brilliant cover designer, Gina, my miracle-working editor, and Laurence, my mentor who always pushes me forward. Thanks also to Brigitte Kishlar, who has nurtured and supported me in every step of my creativity.

Another massive thank you to all of my incredible friends who have supported me through all my creative craziness: Emma, Eli, David, Ana, Mia, Sofi, Nathan, Santi, Lyla, Ivy, Dani, Ari, Amandy, Scarlett, Halsey, and Summer. I'm especially grateful for Mila and Isa, who always read my latest story with wide eyes and bright hearts. The amount of love and support between our friend group is truly extraordinary!

Thank you, thank you, thank you to everyone. I can't wait for the next adventure in Valaztein!

About the Author

Emilia Ramos Samper is among the youngest people to ever publish a book, having released her debut novel, *Crown of Scales and Wonder*, when she was only ten years old. She is also the first-place winner of the LaPlume Young Writers Contest and the Mary Ann Hutchison Memorial Story Contest. Her short story, *Lady of Sand and Scars*, was published by Owl Hollow Press in the teen author anthology *Gathering the Magic* with a foreword by *Eragon* author Christopher Paolini. Emilia loves theater, singing, and all things creative!

Made in the USA
Monee, IL
22 September 2024